C0268C

WINGATE

03/22

Adults, Wellbeing and Health
Libraries, Learning and Culture

Please return or renew this item by the last date shown.
Fines will be charged if the book is kept after this date.
Thank you for using *your* library.

THE NAKED RANGE

THE NAKED RANGE

Steven C. Lawrence

GUNSMOKE

This hardback edition 2010
by BBC Audiobooks Ltd
by arrangement with
Golden West Literary Agency

ISBN 978 1 408 46291 1

British Library Cataloguing in Publication Data available.

Printed and bound in Great Britain by
CPI Antony Rowe, Chippenham and Eastbourne

ONE

Ben Huntoon, who had stumbled in to his place at the long table half awake and late as usual, increased the pace of his eating when he saw McBride had leaned back in his chair and was licking the cigarette he'd rolled into shape. The big foreman noticed young Huntoon and the slower eaters in the crew hurrying.

"Brazos," he said, "you take the creek south to where it hits Big Bend and swing east from there." And, to the next man, a balding dark-skinned rider with a droopy mustache, "Nate, ride north and follow the boundary around 'til you meet Brazos. Both of you haze back any beef that's drifted in." McBride's voice became explicit. "Remember, you bump into anyone, keep clear of trouble."

"What if we see any o' Crashaw's crowd?" Nat Antrim said, frowning thoughtfully.

A sudden, small silence came around the table.

McBride felt the tension, almost as visible as the smoke from his cigarette, that seemed to reach him from the Arrowhead cowhands. He knew the feeling, had been aware of it often enough these last few weeks. He didn't blame them; if someone from one of the other ranches was determined to fight, trying to stay peaceful would only get them killed.

He leaned his long-boned sinewy body forward in the chair, running the problem quickly through his alert mind. A black-haired man of thirty, Tom McBride had a faint pressure at the corners of his mouth that thinned his lips slightly, holding them habitually grim as he gave every face a slow survey before answering.

"Mister Wellman don't want any trouble," he said, "but don't be a damn fool if..."

He broke off, catching the yelling outside. Ben Huntoon stared. The Mexican cook and Antrim exchanged startled glances. Brazos turned around in his chair, reaching wildly for his Winchester. McBride was on his feet. He swung his gunbelt around him, buckled it and opened the bunkhouse door.

Harry Dean had run down from the house, and McBride almost bumped into him when he came through the doorway.

"Dawson's bin shot!" Dean sputtered, his blocky head motioning behind him. "Send someone fer the doc, quick!"

McBride slowed. "Ben ... get going," he ordered.

Most of the cowhands had passed him, and McBride followed to where they were gathering around the two horses. Dawson's small form was silently bent over, trembling and clinging to his pony's saddle horn. Wellman and his daughter, Helen, were watching from the kitchen window in the rear of the big ranch house.

"Get a blanket," McBride said to Antrim. He went in alongside Miller's horse and could see the dark discoloring around Dawson's shoulder.

Miller faced him. "He's not too bad. Bullet went clean through."

"Hold him. Nate's getting a blanket." McBride saw Wellman coming around the corner of the house. "Who did it?" the foreman asked.

"Don't know. We were eatin' breakfast when someone bushwhacked us."

"Anyone else hit?"

"No. Reno an' Garland are stayin' with the cattle though, case anyone tries gettin' 'em."

6

There was some quick swearing, but most of the men said nothing, simply looking quiet and angry. Wellman pushed his way into the center of the circle. The small crowd closed behind their boss.

"How did this happen?" he asked stiffly.

Miller told him.

"Damn it," the cattleman said, and he swore, "this is too much."

"Lemme through heah." The men made an opening and Antrim came in with the blanket.

McBride spoke softly, his orders direct, projecting his sure confidence in handling this. "Get on the ends... Brazos, Cookie. Take it easy."

Dawson groaned and fluttered his eyes as they lowered him. He'd lost a lot of blood, but the bleeding seemed to have stopped. "Into the bunkhouse," said McBride.

Wellman spoke up, "You can use the house, Tom."

"His bunk's closer, Mister Wellman." The big foreman gently held Dawson's twitching good arm as they moved towards the bunkhouse.

The cattleman stood in the center of the dusty yard, watching until his crew went inside. Lew Wellman was a tall man, wide in the shoulders, and his jeans and jumper and grey-flannel shirt were well worn like his riders for, although past sixty, he still put in a good day's work outside. His eyes always seemed worried: they were now. Gray, and set in wrinkles of weariness, they were hard and appraising as he shivered in the clear early morning air that still held the night chill.

"Harry!"

The huge, muscular cowhand turned from where he was looking through the bunkhouse doorway. "Yuh, Mistuh Wellm'n."

7

"Tell McBride I want to see him inside." He swung around and walked towards the large white ranch house.

Harry Dean stepped into the bunkhouse and went quickly down the long and cluttered room to where the men were crowded. There was some muttering and cursing. On the bunk, Dawson's eyes were opened and he seemed comfortable.

"You'll be all right," McBride was saying. "Cookie'll wash you up, and Doc Ellis'll be here soon."

"Sure...thanks, Tom."

"Beats me what some guys'll go to t'get outa a little work," Antrim said, and Dawson laughed.

A few of the others laughed also, but the humor did little to change the temper of the men. They were fired up, and there was worry and fear blended with their anger. Brazos said something about being damned ready for a fight, now, if this was the result of trying to stay peaceful.

"McBride."

"Yes, Harry."

"Mistah Wellm'n wants t'see yuh inna house."

There was a little silence in the room, broken only by Dawson's heavy breathing. "Nobody leave until I get back," the big foreman said and started along past the line of bunks, moving with an easy and controlled step.

Outside, he walked hurriedly, his long shadow jumping before him in the bright sunlight, grateful for a few minutes to think. He'd done a lot of thinking since things began really coming to a head, yet he hadn't gotten a solution. Damn it, you couldn't just forget a good man like Dawson being bushwhacked. If only they could get one of the

8

rustlers. Just one of them. If it all didn't point so clearly to Arrowhead. But that was all he had—ifs.

Helen Wellman answered his knock. She stood back from the door and let him pass.

"Dad's worked up," she said, worried. "Don't let him start a fight."

McBride grimaced. "That wouldn't do any good."

She nodded, relieved now. A rather thin, straight, fairly tall girl a few years older than the foreman, Helen might be considered pretty if it weren't for her clothes and her constant serious dignity. Motherless since an infant, her father had made her mistress of his house, looking to her every want, but holding her, McBride thought, somehow like a prisoner.

Since she'd come back from school five years ago, no young man had called on her. It was Wellman's possessiveness that irked him, McBride knew, his keeping Helen like this, and his insatiable desire for land ... but Wellman was the best cattleman to work for in Kemp Basin so McBride stopped judging him on a personal basis.

A door opened and Wellman came into the room.

"How's Dawson?" He was wearing a .45 Colt and held a Winchester in his right hand.

"Spilled a lot of blood, but he'll be all right. Lucky."

The cattleman looked at him, the anger of a man whose nerves were already drawn too tight, clear in his face. "Lucky? There's no damn reason why they shot Dawson."

Nodding, McBride said, "We shoot up one of the ranches, it won't help. This is eighty-five, Mister Wellman, not sixty-seven."

"I've taken enough from that crowd," Wellman told him. "They begin shooting my men; they're pushing me too far."

"I'll send Antrim in for Bonham."

Helen said, "Yes. Let the sheriff see what's happened for himself. He's believed everything the other ranchers have said. This'll prove Arrowhead isn't behind all the trouble."

Lew Wellman's expression changed, as though he'd just become aware of his daughter's presence. "You go ahead and finish the housework," he said, his voice a slow drawl. "Don't worry about this."

"Dad, don't start any trouble," she said and glanced at McBride, looking for help. "Once you begin taking the law in your own hands..."

"You go ahead and do your housework." Wellman meant that, his face and manner unpleasant. "Get out now, Helen!"

McBride held his face expressionless, managing to keep his annoyance from showing. Like most of the old timers who'd come into the Basin and fought for and held the land since even before McBride was born, Wellman was a bit too sure of his own judgment, but with Helen it was more than just that. He'd lost his wife in childbirth, then tried to create a double in his daughter. But somehow she'd seemed to have failed him. Snapping at her now, humiliating her, was part of that, McBride thought, for the cattleman could never quite face up to the fact that it was impossible to regain what was lost.

Wellman waited until the door closed behind her. He looked at McBride deliberately, as though he'd made up his mind.

"Look, Tom. If we can get Crashaw to get off our

back, there won't be any trouble. So, you've got to see to it he lets us alone. You understand?"

McBride stared but did not answer, and the awkward silence stretched out until Wellman said sharply, "Well, do you understand?"

"Not how Frank can change things," McBride said evenly.

"Well, he's your brother-in-law."

The foreman nodded.

"Frank's not a kid, Mister Wellman. He figures he's right about things, and just talking to him won't change that."

Wellman's face was unpleasant again. "Damn it, Tom, I'm trying to settle this without trouble." He gestured towards the back of the house. "Dawson's out there with a bullet-hole in him. Something's started now, and I can't just let it ride."

"I'd let Bonham handle it."

"Look at the situation," Wellman said patiently. "For three months now, there's been rustling and slow-elking and burning going on. Whoever's done it is pretty clever, never leaving any trail to follow. And, you know damn well we've lost almost a hundred head ourselves. But because I offered to buy when old man Leighton lost so much and decided to sell, Crashaw and the others got to thinking I was behind everything. The talk's getting worse since I bought out Kingman and Streeter, too. My crew can't go into town without having someone start a fight." Again, he pointed towards the bunkhouse. "And now they've begun bushwhacking my men."

"When Bonham gets the rustlers, everything'll straighten out." McBride said.

11

Wellman was annoyed. "I can lose my whole crew before then." His annoyance changed abruptly to anger. "You're going to talk to Crashaw. Call him off ... or dammit, he'll have a range war on his hands."

"Mister Wellman, this crew aren't gunfighters."

Bluntly, "They can be hired easy enough." He meant that.

McBride shrugged. "I don't know. If you didn't offer to buy out every rancher that's had tough luck, everyone wouldn't turn against you, Mister Wellman. These people have pride, and your offering right away every time makes it look like..."

"To hell with what it looks like." Anger controlled him now. "I've got those ranches strictly legal. You know that. And if anyone else wants to sell, I'll buy, just like any of them'd buy if I had to sell. You know that, too. And, by God, unless Crashaw calls that gang off me, he'll get the trouble he's looking for."

He kept glaring at McBride as he pulled open the top drawer of the table in front of him. McBride was thoughtful, not wanting the job of trying to change Crashaw's mind. For some reason he was afraid of it. He saw that Wellman had taken a box of carbine shells out and laid them on the table.

"I'll ride out to the Double F this afternoon, Mister Wellman."

"You go out right now. First, stop into town and tell Bonham to get out here." He dropped a handful of shells into his back pocket. He was patient again. "Be sure Crashaw understands what I mean."

McBride watched him. "I don't think you should

12

take the men out looking for trouble now," he offered, intoning his warning evenly.

Wellman leaned on the table, his long fingers extended and fingertips together. "We'll ride up to the herd and see if we can pick up a trail," he said, holding his irritation at the unwanted advice in check. "Damned if I won't try to get a bushwhacker. I want every hand ready in fifteen minutes."

"I'll tell them." McBride turned and started to leave, but Wellman's words stopped him.

"You be sure Crashaw understands me."

McBride hesitated. "I will," he said finally.

Wellman nodded. "He'd better understand if he wants things kept in hand," he said.

TWO

The sun was well up into the brassy sky, bearing down with its June heat, bright and hard on the dusty road McBride had followed into Cavanagh. Wellman's emotional words kept recurring to him: *Call him off...or dammit, he'll have a range war on his hands.*

Wellman could mean what he'd said about hiring someone to do his fighting. If the other cattlemen made him fight, he'd bring more trouble into the Basin than people could possibly imagine.

McBride was worried. The confidence in his ability and brains and strength in the handling of anything that came with his foreman's job didn't carry over to something like this. Somehow, he'd have to convince Frank Crashaw not to push Arrowhead.

The plain truth was that any fighting would have to be handled with hired guns. As foreman of Arrowhead, McBride was certain of that. Crashaw would have to see it, too, and he'd have to be the one to tone down.

He rode slowly along Grant Street, past the neat line of houses and New England-style church, reining to the left and heading his black gelding for the jail. In a moment McBride became conscious of the watching town.

The heavy tension that seemed directed at him from the people surprised him, then warned him. It was like the tension he'd felt at breakfast, and he didn't like it.

He tied up and went quickly along the boardwalk to the sheriff's office.

Pop Holmes was sitting whittling in a chair near the unlocked heavy iron door that led to the small cell block. The little, white-haired jailor wiped a wrinkled hand across his sweaty forehead when McBride asked for the sheriff.

"Matt went out to the Lazy S 'bout seven 'clock," he said cooly. "Nearly sixty head killed out there this mornin'."

"Loomis around?"

The old jailor gestured out the doorway. "Deputy's makin' a round of the town," he said, "but you'll proba'ly find him into Dundee's. He added matter-of-factly, "Hear Arrowhead had a shootin' this mornin', too."

"Carl Dawson got hit in the shoulder, Pop."

Holmes glanced at him, knowingly, McBride thought. "Them riders is gettin' real darin', hittin' Lazy S and Arrowhead both the same night." He made no further remark, but just looked down again, engrossed in his whittling.

McBride felt like a scolded child from the old man's talk and actions, and, because of this his irritation grew. Pop had made his own decision concerning what was going on in the Basin, and his judgment was against Arrowhead, and against those who worked there.

He went outside and along the walk towards the saloon. Loungers on the hotel steps still watched him. They looked as though they were waiting for something to happen, he felt. He allowed them a casual glance when he pushed through the high, wide, double doors that had large and fancy "D's" on them, painted gold.

With the curtains drawn, the big room, smelling of malt and stale smoke, was darkly cool. McBride

15

gave the five men playing poker at a front table and the few others lined along the bar a quick survey, seeing that Pat Loomis wasn't among them as he walked forward, his footsteps muffled by the sawdust on the floor. A few turned, looking towards him, and he knew the same feeling was present here, too.

His big shoulders tightened slightly, and the gray eyes narrowed. He pushed his sombrero back on his thick black hair, leaning both elbows on the bar, and nodded to those down the counter.

Will Dundee, a big man gradually going to fat, came and stood opposite McBride and mopped the bar with wide, round strokes.

"Same as usual, Tom?" he said. Then, his voice lower, "They're mad, Tom. Lazy S got burned out last night."

McBride nodded. "Same as usual." He didn't remember old Pop saying anything about Lazy S being burned out, only that sixty head had been killed. He made another slow glance at the others.

He saw how they were, gathered together at the table, looking quiet and doubtful.

Four of them came towards him, nothing openly hostile on their faces. But because he couldn't be sure, he kept both hands up on the bar, letting them see he was well clear of his Colt.

The tallest, a husky rancher named Kingman, who'd been burned out three weeks before, spoke for them all. "Sorry to hear Carl Dawson got shot," he said. And as if explaining, "We heard about it when the doc went out."

"Yuh, Carl's a damned good man," added Evans, a stubby, clumsy cowhand who'd been

Kingman's foreman. More of the men began crowding around. "Sorry," said Alf Paulson. "Hell, a shoulder wound ain't nothin'," a skinny bearded rancher named Barstow put in. "He'll be up and 'round in coupla days."

"How many head they kill?" someone asked.

"None. We had four riders out with the herd."

"None," said Evans casually as he let a blob of tobacco juice go into the spitoon. "You wuz lucky. They finished Michaelson's whole herd."

Barstow said, "Burned him out...barn and house, too."

McBride flipped a silver dollar onto the counter. He could see through to their real meaning and made no attempt to conceal it.

"Funny thing how Wellman figgers things so he has extra men ridin' nights now," said Evans. "He's the only man outguessin' them rustlers."

A sudden, tense silence came at the bar.

"I sent the extra hands out," McBride said, looking at the shorter cowhand, his eyes hard and cold. He smiled, but there was nothing warm or humorous there. "Glad you like the way I handle my crew."

"Smart," said Evans, shrugging his wide shoulders. "You're a smart ramrod, McBride."

"That's how I keep my job." McBride wondered if Evans would keep at him.

Kingman shook his head. "If I'd had more hands, I'd have done something like that. They never would've burned me out."

"Mister Wellman gave you a good price," McBride said, a bit disgusted. Kingman had gotten twice the value of his spread, considering

17

there was no stock and all the buildings were gone. McBride watched him with the hard and cold look. "You want him to sell back to you?"

"Oh, no," Kingman said quickly and looked away from McBride's eyes.

McBride was tempted to go on and show them how over-fair Wellman had been in every case where he'd bought someone out. But he became annoyed with himself for he knew the gesture would be useless. McBride felt nothing towards Kingman, not anger, not sympathy. He'd have run his spread into the ground with a year or two, and it would've gone for taxes or the bank would have gotten it anyway.

"You did all right, then," he said casually. "You won't be rich, but Mister Wellman took good care of you."

"Wellman took damn good care of us," Evans said sharply. "All the way through he took damn good care of us."

Another tense silence came then, as if everyone at the bar had suddenly stopped breathing. Evans was pushing it a little too far, coming right out and throwing it at McBride like that. Kingman edged in between the two foremen, chancing a quick glance at McBride. One or two of the watchers edged back, others stirred and felt their faces. Careful men, they knew that pushing the Arrowhead foreman was dangerous any way you tried it.

Alf Paulson broke the prolonged silence. "Well, Tom, good prices or not, there's a lot of us in this basin who'll never sell."

McBride looked at him. He knew all about Paulson's ranch, just as he knew all about every inch of land in the Basin. The hard-working Swede had close to the poorest cattle land around, and he'd sweated blood keeping it going. Wellman would have no use for his spread.

"No reason why you'd have to sell, Alf," he said.

"Well, I've had an offer," Paulson said. "Wellman's offered me twice the value of my place. "He's got no use for my land, Tom. Why's he want it?"

McBride couldn't answer that.

"He's land-crazy," Evans said hotly. "He wants to own this whole damn basin."

The watchers stirred uneasily, each careful and quiet.

Tom McBride turned to Evans and said quietly, "There are some loud-mouths talking it up that Arrowhead's got something to do with all the trouble around here. And I'm Arrowhead's ramrod. So, if you want to be one of the loud-mouths, you just say what you think to me."

Evans looked sharply at that, but Kingman spoke before him. "No one's talking against you, Tom."

McBride hesitated, annoyed with himself for letting the rancher try to talk around him. He noticed that Pat Loomis had come in and was standing behind Paulson. He swallowed a dryness in his throat.

"Anyone talks against Arrowhead talks against me," he said. Now, he looked at Loomis. "And, I don't think there's any law against Mister Wellman buying any ranch that's up for sale, is there, Pat?"

"No law 'gainst it atall," the deputy said. A stringy man, slightly bent, Loomis had been a lawman here for longer than ten years, and people respected him. "Spec'lly since Lew's payin' double price fer everythin' he buys."

"Hell, places keep burnin' like they have been," someone in the back said loudly, "all's he'll end up with is naked range."

Loomis said bluntly, "And, I'd say what Lew buys is his own business."

"I'll send Pop out to the Lazy S in the buggy to tell Matt," said Loomis to McBride.

McBride knew everyone was listening. "Make sure he goes, Pat. We don't want people thinking we're telling stories."

"Sure." Loomis knew what he was driving at. He smiled. "Sure, Tom."

Turning back to the bar, McBride swallowed the last of his drink. "See you around," he said to no one in particular, and started to go.

Paulson's voice stopped him. "Tom, I don't know who's to blame for all the trouble," he said, "but we're going to fight it."

McBride knew that the old Swede wasn't trying to start trouble. He hadn't made a threat, but his strong sense of pride had forced the statement out of him.

"We're fighting it at Arrowhead, too, Alf," he said.

Paulson's white face was strained. "Well, that's how it is, Tom. Once we find out who is to blame, we fight."

McBride nodded, then felt the tension dissolve as he spoke. "I've got a crew including a rider named Dawson that would like a call if you find out first, Alf. You remember that," he said.

THREE

An hour later, McBride's black crossed the shallow creek that bordered the Double F on the north and followed its course for a while until he began breasting the slope of the flat above the ranch buildings. A comfortable breeze faintly pushed along the top of the thick, sun-dried grass.

He approached the sprawling buildings from the left, moving slowly through a long thicket of scrub willow, spotted here and there by fairly lofty cottonwoods or alders, before breaking into the small meadow that ran down almost to the Crashaw home.

McBride saw no movement about the L-shaped ranch house or bunkhouse or barn, but he knew someone would be there. Actually, he hadn't planned just what he'd say, knowing you couldn't plan on anything with Frank, or Frances for that matter.

He got down and gave the rein a couple of idle turns. There was a movement at the corner of the house. He looked. Frances stood there, wearing faded levis and one of Frank's blue shirts, holding a carbine pointed at him.

"What do you want, Tom?" his sister said.

"Why the gun, Franny?"

"Frank don't want me takin' any chances when he's not here." She was as tall as her brother, with the same strength in her sharp, handsome face. Her tone was cold, unfriendly. "That means with everyone."

They're too scared, McBride thought. "Franny, I'm your brother, remember?"

"You ride for Arrowhead. That might change things."

McBride shook his head. "Well, put that damn thing down. Where's Frank, anyway?"

"Rode over to see Ed Linford 'bout two hours ago."

"Ed Linford?"

She had lowered the gun but did not come close to him. "You know Linford. He bought the Crockett place last year."

"How long since Frank's been so close to settlers?" McBride said, his tone hard and sarcastic.

Frances Crashaw was silent for a few moments. "Ed's not a settler. He's got fourteen head now. Besides, some of the settlers are mighty nice people to know."

"I'll have to find out sometime," he said, still stiffly. Then, trying to lighten things, he glanced around. "Place looks good, Franny. Frank kept it up good."

"Why do you want to see him," she said. "We've already turned down Wellman's offer, so..."

"Look, I've got nothing to do with his land buying. What in hell's so strange about me wanting to visit my family?"

After a pause, she said, "It's just that there's been so much trouble, Tom. You don't know who's to blame?"

"Well, you don't think I am, do you?"

"No. Of course not, Tom." She came close and passed him, going up the steps. Her tone was light now. "Come in and have a bite before you go on."

He nodded at clouds that rolled towards the basin, completely covering the Lodestones and darkening the western horizon. "No, thanks. I'd like to get to Linford's before the storm breaks."

"Maybe you'll ride back with Frank, then?"

"Maybe...but I'll ride over some Sunday soon, Franny. Spend the day with you."

Her voice was warm. "We'd like that fine, Tom."

He rode south, for the Linford place lay in the edge of a small meadow in the foothills of the valley. He tried to discount Franny's initial unfriendliness. Although he was six years older than her, they'd been close as twins. Especially after he'd brought his father back, wounded, following the fight with the settlers on the Big Bend. They'd still stayed close during the next four years she'd taken care of the crippled old man, even though Tom only got home on weekends, occasionally, once he began riding for Wellman because there was more money that way. But, naturally, her marriage had changed that. And, just as naturally, her loyalty was only with whatever Frank decided.

Frank and Franny had been good about the old man, McBride thought, staying on the ranch and treating him so fine until he died. And Frank had done a wonderful job of keeping it up, perhaps better than he could've himself if he'd decided to keep ownership. And, because McBride felt close to them, his resentment and doubt continued to bother him, although he understood it was part of the tension and fear he'd seen wherever he went.

Even now he was seeing it. As he kept to the winding run of the willow and alder-fringed creek, he'd passed three small herds of cattle at watering spots and in little meadows, all guarded by more men than usual, mostly familiar faces. Yet the hazy glint of the darkening daylight reflected from the guns they held.

The damp wind coming down off the mountains was penetrating, chilling him. He stopped to let the black gelding drink where the trail turned and dipped into an opening among lines of willows and alders. He sat there, watching lightning streaks over the Lodestones and listening to the thunder.

He was lighting a cigarette, figuring there'd be ample time to have a smoke before the storm hit, when a lone rider broke through the scrub at the far end of the glade.

The rider pulled up, his hand going down and yanking out his scabbarded rifle. Tom's hand brushed against the Colt holstered at his right side.

Now he could tell the rider was Frank Crashaw.

Frank held the carbine out as he came closer, his broad-shouldered body sitting straight in the saddle. Then, when he recognized McBride, he slid the weapon back into place, smiling awkwardly, and offered his hand.

"Can't take chances these days, Tom."

McBride tightened his hand on his brother-in-law's firm grip. "Nobody seems to think so, anyway," he said.

"Franny tell you where I was?" Frank Crashaw was about McBride's age, a shade taller and more solidly built. His clear and honest face looked tired.

McBride nodded. "I was hoping you'd still be at Linford's," he said, after a quick glance skyward. "Looks like it'll be a bad one."

"Well, we can get back there 'fore it hits," Crashaw suggested.

"Sure thing." McBride waited until Crashaw

had turned his sorrel mare and then moved the black in beside him.

"What's on your mind?" said Crashaw, staring at McBride earnestly.

Right to the point, as usual, McBride thought. "You've got to call the ranchers off Arrowhead. They're getting all worked up over nothing."

"I wouldn't call it nothin'."

"It is as far as Arrowhead's concerned," McBride said. "Damn it, Mister Wellman's about at the end of his patience. Dawson's getting shot really got him."

Crashaw turned in the saddle. "Dawson get shot?" he said sharply.

"This morning. In the shoulder, but it's enough to start real trouble."

"So...I'm sorry Carl got shot, but that don't have anythin' to do with me."

"It wasn't rustlers that done it, Frank. It was a whacker."

Silence for a moment. "And you think someone from one of the ranches shot him?"

"Who else?" McBride said dryly. "It could make you all have something bad on your hands."

"We could handle it."

McBride stared at him for a few seconds, feeling the black's shoulders stiffen as they started down to cross the shallow waters of the creek.

Crashaw said, "You think we'll get licked? You think we're just like that bunch of disorganized settlers when they tried to cross Big Bend?"

"I'm telling you you're all wrong about Mister Wellman, Frank. He's not behind the killing and burning. You've got to stop the ranchers from rustling Arrowhead stock."

25

"You've got no proof who's been taken' your cattle."

McBride looked at him knowingly. "We tracked six heads into Griffith's corral. Mister Wellman did the old fool a favor not pressing charges."

Crashaw said nothing.

"You've got to bring in the man who shot Dawson, Frank."

"Just like that," said Crashaw bitterly. "You're givin' me an ultimatum, and I've got to obey."

Both of them were getting irritated, and McBride knew an out and out argument wouldn't settle anything. Frank couldn't see his side of the simplest things, especially around the ranch, just as though he and Franny were afraid he'd claim title to the land.

He held back his fury. "Frank, Wellman's ready to give you a range war if you push him any farther."

"If I push him," Crashaw said, his big fist tightening on the rein. He glanced angrily at McBride, his bitterness out in the open. "That damned land-vulture you work for is behind the whole damned thing, Tom. I don't know how you can work there and not see it."

A deep clap of thunder sounded and McBride looked ahead. The flat that ran to Linford's was still beyond the trees, but he figured they'd beat the rain.

Crashaw's mood had softened, partly because of McBride's silence. "Look, Tom," he said seriously. "I know you can't do anything about Wellm'n. You can't even talk up to him and keep your job. But he's out to get control of the Basin, and he's behind the trouble. He's always Johnny-on-the-spot, money in his hand, when someone's place gets hit.

There's only one way we can lick him, and that's to get so damn strong he won't dare go any further."

"He'll go farther than you think."

Smiling crookedly, Crashaw said, "Well, we're strong enough to handle anythin' Arrowhead can cause."

"Look, Frank, what about Franny?"

"We've talked it over, and she's agreed on standing up. Arrowhead ain't too big, y'know."

"Frank, if it comes to a fight, hired guns'll do Mister Wellman's fighting," McBride said bluntly.

Crashaw stared at him, breathing heavily. "We've got law in this basin. Bonham wouldn't stand for that."

"It would get too big for him. Can't you see that?"

Watching Crashaw's confused face, McBride realized he should let him think about it. The fact that his attitude had shifted was promise enough.

They broke from the trees onto the sloping flat that ran to the Linford ranch.

Linford stood on the porch now, staring down across the meadows at the riders. He held a carbine ready, McBride could see. He slowed his black as they went through a gate in the barbed wire fence.

Once past the fence, they opened into a trot. Linford raised his hand and waved when they were halfway across the meadow. He shifted the gun to the crook of his oddly bent right arm and waited, his only movement a turn of his head as though he was talking to someone inside.

When they reined in, he came down the steps holding the right arm stiff and bent, a leathery-faced man in his fifties, with a nearly-white mustache and grizzled white hair.

"Thought you'd be comin' back, Frank, with

this storm blowin' down so quick." He nodded to McBride, studying him with interest.

"You know Franny's brother Tom, Ed," said Crashaw.

"I know him," the rancher said. "Look, put your mounts into the barn. It'll hit any minute."

McBride knew Linford was taking his measure, but he showed nothing on his face as he began following Crashaw into the barn.

"Obliged, Mr. Linford," he said, aware of the resentment here, and the reason for the deliberate appraisal. Tom McBride's part in the fight at Big Bend was well-known. Linford had gotten that game arm there, when he'd tried to cross with the rest of the settlers; and at that, he was one of the lucky ones, coming out of it with only a crippled arm.

A sudden great booming of thunder shook the building as he turned to leave and the rain struck, the downpour pounding loudly, as if spilling from huge buckets, onto the boarded roof.

They ran for the house, the fishtailing wind and splattering rain cold, and chilling McBride to the bone. Linford stood near the doorway, watching him, still frowning, obviously not pleased he'd come.

"Lucky I bumped into Tom," said Crashaw casually. "Glad I'm not out in that."

"Shouldn't last too long," Linford said, still making no motion to go inside. He didn't want McBride in his house, and Crashaw saw that.

Now, a great fork of zigzagging lightning stabbed out of the overhead darkness, crashing somewhere in the foothills, shaking the house. Beneath the rolling of thunder a moment later,

McBride caught the squeaking of a door opening. He glanced up absently, listening to the gusting pound of the rain, and he saw the girl standing behind Linford.

"I told you to stay inside," he heard the rancher say in a low voice."

The girl looked frightened. It was the thunder and lightning that had forced her out, McBride knew, but she made no excuse. When she noticed McBride watching her, she looked back boldly, her lips a tight line across her tanned thin face. She was perhaps twenty, wearing jeans and a worn blue shirt; her brown hair that was parted in the middle was cut boyishly short. Her brown eyes were steady, almost arrogant.

"This is my daughter Susan, McBride," said Linford.

McBride smiled and the girl nodded, resentment still on her face.

"I've seen you in town," McBride said.

She watched him gravely. "I've heard of you," was all she said. Then, she looked skyward at the rocketing glare of a lightning flash.

The girl shivered, and she smiled briefly when she saw Crashaw's eyes watching her, too. "Close," he said, grinning.

Linford had crossed to the end of the porch, moving quickly, leaning against one of the square timber supports with his bad arm.

Turning, Linford said, "Somethin' got hit." He pointed to a billowing column of black smoke rising above the trees. It was a big fire.

Crashaw was beside him now. "I'd say it's Alf Paulson's place."

"Think we should go?" Linford spoke the

question guardedly, as if he hadn't wanted McBride to hear.

"Yes," said Crashaw. "I'll get the horses."

Linford turned to his daughter. "Get some slickers out. And get my belt." And when McBride started towards the barn, "No, I'll bring your mount. I want to talk to Frank alone."

They're worse than Wellman, McBride thought, watching the two men running to the barn. At least Arrowhead is making a try at understanding.

He turned, hearing the door squeak again, and saw Susan coming out with her father's gunbelt and the slickers. She held one out to him. "No need of your getting wet," she said more friendly than before.

"Thanks." His mind worked quickly, sharply. She could give him the information about Crashaw's coming here, but she wasn't stupid and he'd have to be careful. "Your father likes to keep secrets."

"He's got reason to," she said quietly, her voice tight again.

McBride leaned against a porch pole and studied her, bewildered at the sudden change. "Look," he said calmly, "lots of people are too jumpy these days."

"Wellman won't get this place," she said. "We want no part of anyone who has anything to do with him."

Her attention had shifted to her father and Crashaw coming from the barn. He put on the slicker, then stepped off the porch and took the bridle from Linford. The old man stayed behind to say something to Susan, and McBride and Crashaw moved off together across the meadow.

McBride glanced back, but he could only see vague shadows through the wall of rain. The black's speed was held up by the hoof-deep mud, and McBride was forced to give all his attention to holding him, for he'd be startled into sudden fits of snorting and bucking when the blinding red-hot sheet lightning crashed close up.

In another half-hour, when they broke from a line of willow into a wide, deep-earthed flat of water-drenched grass, they saw that it was Paulson's barn that had been struck.

The ranch, snuggled among a cluster of alders, was well-kept with its small neat house and long corral behind the barn. McBride could see the barn was almost completely gutted. Heavy black smoke stinking of roasted meat billowed up to the sodden sky. In front of the house, a line of men passed buckets from the well to those fighting the dying blaze.

The riders reined in near the half-dozen men standing at the well. McBride sucked in a deep breath. Neighbors helping out in a fire, he'd expected, but he saw now that this was more than that. There were both ranchers and settlers present, and every man heavily armed, every scabbard holding a rifle. And, from the way he was stared at and watched, he knew he wasn't welcome here either.

"Who in hell asked for Arrowhead's help?" the slow-moving stubby cowhand named Evans asked when Crashaw dismounted.

Crashaw became annoyed. "Keep your mouth shut. Tom's along to give a hand, too." And when Evans still eyed him sharply. "Everything all right with Alf?"

"He was inside the barn when it got hit," one of the men told him. "Can't get in yet to get 'im out."

"What about his wife?"

Evans gestured towards the house. "Barstow's in takin' care of her. She got her han's burned tryin' t'get inside."

McBride got into the bucket-line. The storm was lessening. And, because the wind wasn't fanning the blaze, better progress was made, allowing the men to move inside the charred remains.

A call came down the line for Crashaw, and McBride saw those up front beginning to crowd around something in the ruins. At first he was going to follow the men who went with Crashaw but then he saw how they were, all gathered together, some staring back at him, looking quiet and angry.

They were worked up all right, so much they resented even his helping. Probably Wellman couldn't keep out of a fight, no matter how hard he tried, not with this attitude so strong on the other side.

"Tom, come up here," Crashaw called.

There was a movement and muttering among the crowd as McBride walked forward. He noticed that Barstow had come to the door of the house and now stood talking to those grouped there.

"I don't give a damn," Evans was arguing with Crashaw, "he was in Dundee's this mornin', an' that gives him plenty time t' send word back."

McBride came abreast them. Suddenly, Evans reached out and grabbed the shoulder of his slicker, the force of the grasp pushing McBride, making him slide in the mud. Crashaw pulled

Evans back, swearing loudly at him as he shoved him away from McBride.

"What the hell?" McBride said. His hard, cold eyes watched Evans for another movement.

"Get back! Get back!" Crashaw ordered. Then, he motioned to McBride. "You have a look at this."

McBride followed him into the ruins. The stinking smoke was sharp in his nostrils, bringing tears to his eyes. McBride saw the figure lying there on the ground, and, looking closer, he had a sudden weak feeling in his legs and stomach as if he were going to vomit. There was only half a man lying there. Paulson's face was a charred, bloody mess, so you knew who it was, but his legs and right arm and part of his body was torn away.

"Lightnin' didn't do that," someone said.

And Evan said quickly, "I'd say it was dynamite."

There was some muttering now, more curses, and the disturbance began to spread.

McBride stared at Crashaw. "You can't blame Arrowhead for this," he said. "Good Lord, you don't think Mister Wellman'd do anything like this?"

More mumbling, swearing. He knew he'd started wrong. There were jeers, and men waved their weapons. Then, suddenly, they quieted as one, and McBride looked around and saw that Paulson's wife had come into the crowd.

She was a small, graceful woman with a tired face and calm eyes, and her expression didn't change as she stared down at her husband's body. She simply made a hopeless gesture with her head and turned to go.

Crashaw said to her, "Mrs. Paulson, did Alf have any dynamite in the barn?"

The woman shook her head.

"Could he have had some there without your knowing?"

"No." And, as if it was very important, "He was going to get some though. To root out them oak stumps in the south meadow. Mistah Harding at the bank was givin' us a loan to fix the place up . . ."

A loud voice cut her off. "Hey, anyone here come in from 'hind the bahn?" It was one of the settlers.

Silence. Then, some mumbling began. "I came in through the corral," Barstow said.

"But, you didn't stop 'hind the bahn."

"No."

"Well, theah's tracks out theah," the dungareed man said, looking at Linford. "Think it's worth a try?"

Linford turned to Crashaw. "What you think?"

"We'll try it," Frank Crashaw said. And at that, men went for their horses.

McBride walked back to the well and got up onto his black. The lightning had stopped and only a drizzly rain still came from the overcast sky. Most of the men were mounted and had begun to form a circle with Crashaw and Linford in the center. McBride moved into the rear of the gathering, picking his way past some settlers.

Barstow saw his waiting, and he said, "Where's he going?"

Crashaw was cautious. "Who?"

"McBride."

"Yuh," Evans put in, "we don' want nobody from Arra'head 'long. 'Specialy him."

"Tom's good at trackin'," Crashaw said.

"Who in hell wants him 'long," Evans flared, "when he could be the one respons'ble for this."

"What're you talkin' about," Crashaw said. "Tom was with me and Ed Linford when this happened."

"So...he couldn't't've helped set it up?" Evans looked around the line of faces and saw agreement there. "McBride heard Alf say this mornin' he wouldn't sell. He could've sent word to Wellman."

The inference shocked McBride. And, because most of these men had been his friends, he looked around, studying their serious faces, to see how they felt. Their mouths were hard and eyes nervous and bright, and none would stare him in the eye.

"Well," Evans said, "I say he don't come."

Crashaw shook his head. "We don't want anyone from Arrowhead along, Tom," he said.

McBride nodded without comment. Now, he suddenly straightened in the saddle and began pulling his horse away, then angled across the yard back the way he'd come.

FOUR

McBride followed the trail running along the creek. Twice he halted to listen for sound in his back trail, making sure one of the more violent and doubtful riders back there hadn't followed him with a twisted idea of squaring things up for Alf Paulson.

He had failed to hold Frank Crashaw completely, which would really give Wellman the go-ahead on getting ready for a fight. There was more at stake now than just losing a few head and maybe a building being burned.

Crashaw had everything set up, with everyone in the Basin lined up against Arrowhead, including the settlers. They looked like a well-trained company of cavalry, no longer a peaceful group bent on protecting their land, but one spoiling for a fight.

There was still a chance of holding back an out-and-out war. With the settlers out of it, Crashaw might think twice and give Bonham time to clear things up. He reined to the left, forded the river at a riffle, and headed for the Linford ranch.

Susan Linford could be the tool to hold back her father, one that might keep the settlers out of it. Frank Crashaw had been clever to bring Linford in with him, using the former settler as his go-between them and his ranchers.

McBride made his plan sensibly and coldly. Remembering the girl's fear of the storm, he would draw a much worse picture for her about a range war. And, thinking of her father's arm, he knew she could be reminded of the fight at Big Bend.

Give it to her with a little build-up, he thought. Magnifying it wouldn't really be lying. Crashaw would fight according to decent rules, and Linford would follow only where he believed himself in the right. That would be wonderful except for the fact that the men Wellman would bring in wouldn't follow any set of rules. And everyone would see that their brand of force was far worse than what had happened at Big Bend.

When he was half-way across the meadow, passing the few head of stocky white-faces bearing the Linford brand the girl must have brought out after the storm, he saw a movement in one of the windows.

The door opened when he entered the yard and an unsmiling Susan Linford came out. She held a Winchester that seemed almost as big as her small body. She looked boyish, standing there in shirt and jeans, with nothing friendly in her frosty stare.

"Why'd you come back?" she said.

He reached down and took the slicker from the saddle horn. "Rain's over. Thought I'd return this." And, gesturing towards the carbine, "Point that thing another way, will you. Makes me nervous."

She hesitated a moment, and said finally, "Where are Frank and Dad?"

"They'll be along soon. Alf Paulson died in the fire, and they rode out looking to see if it could've been set."

Silently she studied him.

"Look," he said, "I'd like to talk to you."

"We have nothing to talk about."

"Yes, we have. It concerns your father and what

37

can happen in this basin. Unless people get smart and stop hunting for a fight."

"Arrowhead's the only one looking for a fight," she said, her voice tightening.

"Look, I'm not here to argue," he said. "Unless you want your father brought back to you hanging down over a saddle, you'd best hear me out. Now, do we talk?"

There was a silence. Then, she lowered her weapon. "Well?" she said.

"Not here. Inside. I'm too much of a target out here."

"No one's going to shoot you."

"Not if I'm careful, they won't. Do I come in?"

She watched him for a moment and, without saying anything, turned and opened the door. He followed her inside.

"Thanks for trusting me."

"Did I have a choice?" she said flatly.

The long living room was pleasant, nicely furnished with matched chairs and table, and dainty white curtains at the windows.

"You people've fixed this place up nice," he said.

"For settlers" she said distantly. "You said you wanted to talk about my father."

McBride took off his sombrero and laid it on a chair. "Relax," he said. "You can't think things out if you're not relaxed." She made no answer, her stare was still cold, and he went on. "There's a good chance there'll be a big fight in the Basin. And your father's going to get caught right in the middle of it."

"I know that. And I know Arrowhead's to blame for it all."

"Well, you know wrong, then," he said angrily.

"You've been sold the same story as your father. And he might damn well get himself shot at because of it."

Her chin went up. "He got shot at in Big Bend."

"This'll be lots worse than Big Bend," he said. "Both sides lined up there and fought it out. We held the river fair and square..."

She broke in, "And you made a big name for yourself leading the charge that drove us back across to the south side."

"I'm not here to talk about that," he said hotly. "I just want you to realize your father'll probably get killed fighting Wellman. Damn it, you should realize we're not gunfighters at Arrowhead. My crew's cowhands, nothing more. And if Wellman's forced to fight, he'll hire gunslicks to do it for him."

Susan stared at him, the color of her face draining from her cheeks.

"Wellman'll turn this range into a hell for everyone," he said, purposely trying to be cruel. "He's not behind all the trouble and people are throwing everything at him. He's got a right to be mad. And, he'll be merciless." He gestured towards the meadow. "You people are all alone out here. They could kill your father easy when he's out with his herd."

He waited at her silence, studying her face, now tense with concern and fear.

"How can I do anything?" she said.

"You're Ed Linford's daughter," he said coldly. "You can talk him out of fighting Arrowhead. You can keep him alive." Knowing her thoughts, "Look, he's at the head of the settlers, isn't he?"

"Yes."

"Well, if he quits, they'll quit." His voice was

calmer now, logical. "And, if Crashaw loses half his supporters, he'll let the sheriff handle the trouble."

She shook her head slowly.

"You've got to decide," he said.

McBride studied her with narrowed eyes. "Well, what do you say?"

She shook her head again wearily. "I don't know. I really don't know what to do."

There would be only one decision, he knew, after she thought about it. "You've got to try. You've got to do what's right."

"Yes, I know."

He opened the door and went outside. She followed. He mounted the black and looked down at her.

"Well," he said, "I've done all I could."

She nodded slowly.

Susan looked across the meadow, a tight frown wrinkling her smooth forehead. Her eyes were warmer. "You'll try to stop Wellman, won't you?"

"I'll do everything I can to stop a fight," he said. Then, he started the black across the flat, opening him up immediately.

It was almost eight when he got back to Arrowhead, and by then the evening had turned comfortably cool. As he drew the black to a halt, he could see Harry Dean standing outside the bunkhouse door waiting for him.

"You took long 'nuff," the huge man said. He strolled across the yard to where McBride had dismounted near the barn. He seemed nervous as well as business-like. "The boss wants t' see yuh."

"Soon as I take care of Cloud," McBride said.

Dean stepped in close to him, his powerful body

40

bent a little. "Mistah Wellm'n said he wanted t'see yuh soon's yuh got back. Yuh know them's orders. C'mon, Tom. Boss ain't inna good mood. We saw someone burned all our buildings up at the line camp last night, too. C'mon an' hurry."

So they've started burning Arrowhead property now, McBride thought. Damn fools! That's what Crashaw and the rest were, damn fools.

Wellman was waiting in the living room, sitting behind his long mahogany desk.

"Well, what'd he say?" the rancher asked bluntly.

"The idea of hired guns had him worried," said McBride. "But Alf Paulson's getting killed got him fired up."

"Alf Paulson?"

"Someone dynamited his barn during the storm. He was inside."

"And, he's dead," Wellman said, his voice low. Suddenly he stood: "Oh, damn it! Damn that happening!"

"Crashaw found a trail and followed it," McBride said.

Quickly. "Did they find anything?"

"I didn't go along with them. Arrowhead isn't wanted no matter what happens. Crashaw had enough cowhands and settlers with him to..."

Wellman broke in. "Settlers?"

"Crashaw's got them with him now. He's got Ed Linford to get them to take his side." Immediately, he wished he hadn't mentioned Linford's part in it at all.

The tall rancher stared at him, the gray eyes showing nothing. McBride didn't know whether he was thinking of Paulson or the settlers; it was

41

impossible to guess accurately how deeply Wellman could feel about another man's dying, no matter how brutal, when his mind was centered on his land.

Finally, Wellman said, "Harry tell you the line camp was burned out?"

McBride hadn't expected a sudden shift like that. He nodded.

"I don't know why those fools don't see I'm getting as bad as them," said Wellman. "Well, they've gone too far."

"You can't be sure it's the ranchers, Mister Wellman."

"It is, damn it. And I don't care how many of them they've got. They'll get a fight." He pointed a long finger at McBride as though demanding he understand. "I've got every bit of land I own, legally. Never broke a law. You know that. But now I'm going to fight them."

"But the settlers might drop out," McBride said. He told the rancher about his talk with Susan Linford. "Once the nesters are out of it, Crashaw won't dare fight," he offered. "He'll have to wait until Bonham finds out who's behind everything."

He watched Wellman, his eyes questioning.

"You think that'll work, Tom?" Wellman said, rubbing his chin. "You think if the settlers drop out, Crashaw'll lay off?"

"He'd have to."

Wellman said slowly, "I don't want trouble, Tom. But I'm worried about things." He swung around to Dean, who had stood just inside the doorway during the entire talk. "Someone might get trigger-happy and try to do me or Helen some damage. So, I'm having Harry, here, move into the house. I'm not taking any chances."

McBride felt a sharp surge of hope at that. Wellman didn't really want a fight any more than Crashaw. The foreman felt glad that the rancher's concern for his daughter and himself dominated the shrewd, tough business-man side of him. He said quietly, "I don't blame you, Mister Wellman," and turned to go.

The rancher's words stopped him. "We'd better get two more hands in here for awhile, Tom. One to take Harry's place, and one for Carl Dawson, until his arm's better."

"I don't know who we can get," McBride said, watching him, thinking, and more hopeful now, for Wellman knew any man he'd bring in wouldn't be a hired gun. "You won't get a rider in this basin."

Wellman considered that, and then he said to Dean, "Can you think of anyone, Harry?"

Dean shrugged his huge shoulders. "Tom's right, Mistah Wellm'n." He started to follow McBride to the door but stopped before he'd taken three steps. "I could ride over to Jensen Hole and see if anyone'd want to come here for a little while."

"How about that, Tom?" said Wellman.

"Sure. But I'd like to talk to anyone he brings in before you hire them."

"Of course, Tom," said Wellman. "We'll do it the way we've been doing it." He breathed in deeply and, somehow, McBride felt the rancher was relieved, too, happy to have some hope of still keeping out of a fight.

FIVE

McBride got up earlier than usual the next morning and sat at the table smoking a cigarette while the Mexican cook made breakfast. He nodded to Brazos and Miller, who came in a short while later, saying nothing to them. When Antrim entered, he walked to where the foreman sat.

Antrim fingered his droopy mustache and glanced around at the others briefly. "Like t' talk t' yuh, Tom," he said.

"Sure...go ahead," McBride said, taking in a deep drag and exhaling the smoke slowly.

"Mind comin' outside," the dark-skinned cowhand said.

"What's wrong with here, Nate?"

"It's somethin' personal. I dohn want no trouble, Tom."

McBride was becoming annoyed. Antrim was a lanky but powerfully built man, slightly bald at thirty-five, and one of the best men in the Arrowhead crew. He was a worrier, though, and he often bothered McBride with his troubles.

"All right, what's up, Nate?"

"Yuh heard 'bout the line camp bein' burned out?" Antrim said in a low voice.

He began to smile but saw Antrim was scared. There was no cowardly bone in the cowhand's body, and it was significant that he'd be frightened. "It don't take any guts to burn out an empty line camp," he said to him.

"Mebbe not. But I'm quittin', Tom."

He stared at Antrim, doubtfully. "Nate, you

44

knew damn well the camp'd be the first place hit."

"What 'bout Carl gettin' shot?"

"Look," McBride said, standing straight and studying the cowhand with his hard eyes, "you know you'll never get another job in the Basin with all the trouble on. And, the boss'll see to it you don't get hired within a hundred miles if you quit when things get tough."

Antrim nodded and said after a minute, "I'll take my chances."

McBride was watching him closely. "You talked to any of the crew about this."

"No." He shrugged his wide shoulders and made a weak gesture with his hands. "You've been a good rod heah, Tom, but I don' und'stan' why yuh stick with the boss. Don' let Wellman use yuh as a messenger boy with the otha ranchers."

The foreman's mouth tightened along the corners. "What're you driving at, Nate?"

"Can't yuh see it. You're Wellman's buffer 'tween him and Crashaw. He knows Frank'll never hit the spread hard while you're workin' hard. And, he'll keep yuh tryin' t'hold Crashaw down 'till he's the last other owner in the Basin."

"So, you're giving me warning," McBride said, smiling slightly.

"Tom, I'm tired of watchin' Wellman ridin' on everyone else's tough luck." Antrim's face was concerned. "And I hate t' see him usin' yuh. Hell, Tom, you could git a job anywhere as rod, an' you know it."

McBride was silent a few seconds. It would be a relief, he thought, to have only his foreman's job on his mind. He knew his constant edginess was due to his concern for the Crashaws and those who'd be hurt if it came to a battle; but he couldn't simply ride out and let things go from bad to worse.

"Use yuh head," Antrim said, watching the foreman's thoughtful face closely. "And listen t' me, Tom. Wellman wants every inch of land heah and he's goin' to fight if he has to. Once the shootin' starts youh'll have t'take his side."

McBride looked at him sharply. He'd have to take part in it himself. He knew it.

"You think 'bout it," Antrim said. "But, remember what I said. And, why I'm quittin'."

"You'd better get out today, then," McBride said thoughtfully. "I'll get your pay from the boss."

McBride went inside, but now he didn't feel like eating his usual meal. Everyone was quiet this morning, with the same tension present. McBride glanced from face to face, aware that they weren't meeting his eyes purposely.

Harry Dean came in noisily. When the cook set a long platter of eggs in front of his plate, he said, "Nothin' fer me." The huge man stopped behind the foreman. "McBride, Mistah Wellm'n wants t' see yuh up at the house, rite away."

Looking cautiously around, McBride saw the brooding expressions on the faces, some of the crew trying to act as though they hadn't heard. But, when Dean said that the sheriff was at the ranch house, every head came up.

"What's that got to do with me?" McBride asked, not hiding the sarcasm in his voice.

"Boss jest said to get yuh. Sed it was important."

He rose listlessly and went to the door. Opening

46

it, he saw Bonham had left the house and was walking his stallion across the yard towards the back trail down to the road. The sheriff reined in and waited for McBride to reach him.

"Sorry I missed you in the office yesterday, Tom," Bonham said.

"You got out here, anyway, Matt."

Bonham leaned forward on the saddle horn, his thin body completely alert.

He had been sheriff in the county since a month after the battle in Big Bend, a small man in the late forties, quiet-spoken but as hard and ruthless when he had to be as the Navy Colt he wore.

"You were at the fire at Paulson's?" Bonham asked.

"Yes...damn shame."

"Crashaw and his men followed that trail, and it led right onto Arrowhead land."

"Did they get anyone?"

"No. Smart man. Went into the river. They lost him."

McBride got cautious. "You think it was one of the crew?"

After a moment, the sheriff said, "Whoever it was seemed headed for here. He went onto the river three times. They found the trail twice, but lost it the last time. What do you think?"

"There's no killers in this crew," McBride said quickly.

"You make sure there ain't. You're ramrod here. Nothin's happenin' without you knowin' it."

"Matt, Arrowhead isn't behind the trouble."

Bonham shrugged his small shoulders. "Well, you keep your eyes open. Once I find out who is to blame, I'm comin' after them. Whoever it is, Tom, I'll get them. You think that over." He turned his mount and rode from the yard.

As he went to the house, he wondered how much Bonham had left unsaid. And, he saw that Wellman was deeply concerned about the law man's visit when he entered the living room.

The rancher was standing just inside the door. "I suppose Bonham told you about that trail."

McBride said he had.

Helen Wellman had come into the room.

Wellman looked around now, his eyes dark and furious, but when he saw his daughter, his expression changed immediately. He smiled carefully at her.

"You want something, Helen?"

She took a step timidly forward. "I thought I heard someone arguing in here," she said. She was pale.

"We were just talking," Wellman said. "You go back to your work." He turned away from her as if the affair was settled.

"I saw the sheriff here," she said. "Is there trouble?"

Wellman drew in a deep breath. "Helen, there's nothing to worry about. You go ahead now."

Helen looked at McBride. "Matt was talking to you, Tom. Is he making more trouble for us?"

The rancher's voice got hard for the first time since Helen had entered the room. "Helen, I said there was no trouble. Now, you get back to your work."

She backed towards the kitchen, her eyes still worried, and when she went through the doorway, her father crossed the room and pulled the door tight.

Then, he returned to where McBride stood. "Don't you think I'm being pushed too far?" he asked.

"Too far?"

Wellman nodded, taking a long, slow breath. "First, as soon as the trouble around here started, people began blaming me." He numbered each statement he made by straightening out a finger on his left hand and pointing to it with his right. "My name's been turned into dirt; my cattle have been shot and rustled; my men have been shot; my buildings have been burned; and, someone who's committed a brutal murder sets things up so it looks like Arrowhead did it."

He paused, looking into McBride's eyes; then, "Don't you think it's about time I fought?" he said quietly.

"Bonham didn't make any accusations," McBride said. "Maybe if you talked to Frank Crashaw you could convince him..."

"Talk to Crashaw." Wellman cursed softly. "Tom, I told Bonham if any of that Crashaw crowd came into my land, they'd be shot. And, I expect you to pass that on to my crew."

"What if you went to Frank's place? He'd see you're sincere."

"To his ranch. When?"

"Today."

Wellman grinned contemptuously at him. "I'd be a damned fool to do that. One of those trigger-happy fools would bushwhack me like they did Dawson."

"Not if I'm with you."

Wellman thought about that. "All right," he said, meeting the foreman's eyes directly. "I'll try one more time!"

49

Dean moved to Wellman's side and stood there. McBride remembered something. "Harry'd better get three new hands, Mister Wellman," he said. "Nate Antrim told me he was quitting today."

Wellman had started to take a step foreward, but he stopped. "Well, I'll be damned," he said, breathing heavily. "It's come to that, huh?"

"Hell, Antrim'd be no good in a fight anyways," Harry Dean said unpleasantly. "We won't miss 'im. He..."

The rancher glanced at the big cowhand quickly, his eyes telling Dean to be quiet. Then, Wellman said, "All right, Tom. We'll pay him off. Tell him to pick up his pay before he leaves."

McBride nodded. He was slightly surprised at the casualness in Wellman's voice, and the quiet of his face. He had expected some cursing and hard words for Antrim.

"I'll meet you in the barn," Wellman said after a short pause.

When McBride returned to the bunkhouse to get his sombrero he saw Carl Dawson was already sitting up in his bunk. Dawson waved with his good arm and smiled happily.

"How's the shoulder?" McBride said.

"Com' 'long fine," the little cowhand said. "I'll be back in the saddle inna coupla days."

"Don't rush it," McBride said. He rested his hand on Dawson's boney arm. "Say, Carl, you were around during the storm yesterday. You remember if anyone in the crew was missing?"

"No one was, Tom. Everyone got back from ridin' up to the line camp 'bout half hour 'fore the storm hit." Then, he added quickly. "Everyone 'cept you, Tom."

"How about Harry Dean?"

"Harry was here, too. Him an' Brazos an' the Mex played poker with me 'til the rain let up." He was slightly puzzled. "What's the matter, Tom?"

"Nothing, Carl." McBride started for the door but stopped and looked back at Dawson's little figure lying there. He stared at him and said, "Look, Carl. Keep it quiet 'bout me asking, huh?"

"Sure...sure, Tom," Dawson said.

SIX

After saddling his black McBride waited outside the barn with the grey stallion Ben Huntoon had brought around for Wellman.

When Antrim came out, he looked like he'd been well talked to, walking thoughtful and quickly to the bunkhouse for his warbag. Wellman was close behind him. The rancher said nothing as he mounted and started off at a jog.

They ignored the winding road, taking a more direct route southeastward, moving at a steady pace, crossing the shallow Big Bend at the usual ford three miles below the ranch and then climbing out of the wide flat through which the river ran. McBride sat loosely, studying the view of the entire basin. He noticed Wellman looking around too, frowning slightly, not enjoying the view but studying the land for the presence of a waiting bushwhacker.

The day was clear, the sun with its driving heat, bright in the cobalt sky. They passed small ranches along the winding route, moving through the neighborhood McBride had grown up in, where men worked about buildings and fields in their business of cattle. Children played in yards and sat on corral fences watching and learning.

McBride knew these people, their pride and hopes and beliefs, how unreasonable they were about their disagreements, but he was sure there was a point you could reach with them by way of compromise. There's a chance, with Wellman coming along like this, he thought, as he reined his mount to the right and angled past the large cottonwoods shading the Double F yard.

Frances Crashaw came onto the porch while they were tying up, and McBride was relieved to see she'd left the Winchester inside.

Nodding, he said, "Mister Wellman'd like to talk to Frank."

"He's in the barn."

Wellman turned towards the barn, but Frances stopped him.

"I'll get him. Come inside and wait."

McBride went up the stairs and onto the porch, then held open the door for the rancher before following him into the familiar living room. Franny and Frank hadn't changed much in here during the years he'd been gone. Cleanliness and neatness all around, but nothing new.

Damn it, he hoped they'd be reasonable, seeing Wellman here like this.

He heard the back door close. Frank Crashaw came in wearing a filthy shirt and jeans, his bare arms streaked with dirt and sweat. Only the six-gun he wore was out of place for a man working in his barn. Frances stopped at the doorway and watched.

"I didn't expect you to come alone like this, Wellm'n," Crashaw said.

"Well, I hoped we could talk out our differences, Frank. Try to fight the trouble together."

McBride saw the little frown that came on Crashaw's face. "How do you figger that?" Crashaw said.

"Whoever's causing the trouble has only the Basin to hide in," offered Wellman logically. "If we get all our men together we're bound to close in on them sooner or later."

Crashaw looked worn and bothered, a mixture of hope and doubt apparent in his eyes while he thought about it.

"Would you be willin' t'stop buyin' up every ranch that gits hit?" he said. "And, have your crew give a hand rebuildin'?"

Wellman seemed badgered. "I'm a businessman as well as a rancher, Crashaw."

"You're a neighbor, too. Thet's what the rest of us are doin' for each other. The settlers are in on it, too. You willin'?"

"I think we can lick the trouble together," Wellman said, ignoring the question. "And I'm here for that. What I buy has nothing to do with that."

"I think it does."

McBride could see the tempers rising now. He said to Crashaw. "You should listen to Mister Wellman, Frank. He's being pretty fair about coming here like this."

"Fair 'bout it," Crashaw said slowly. "That's a laugh. I don't see nothin' fair 'bout a man growin' rich on everyone else's tough luck." He looked at Wellman. "I s'pose you're goin' right over to Alf Paulson's spread with your money in your hand."

"I'm here to talk about our business," Wellman said, his voice tense. "That doesn't concern you."

"It does concern me...and everyone else in Kemp Basin."

"Oh, hell," Wellman said angrily. "I was a fool to think you'd listen anyway." He hesitated, then went on in a soft, compromising voice. "You'll hold onto this ranch right up until the end, won't you?"

"We'll keep it 'til it goes for taxes." Crashaw glanced at his wife as he said that.

"Keep off my back. Get out of that gang lined up against me, and you can keep your spread. You just drop out of the whole thing."

Crashaw looked disgusted, angrier. "You mean break up the opposition to you? That's double-crossin' every decent man in the Basin."

"Well, you'll keep your ranch," Wellman said flatly.

"I'll keep it anyway."

Wellman shook his head. He rolled his big shoulders as he turned fully back to Crashaw. "I'll buy up any place that's for sale in this basin." His voice was snappy, hard. "I'll get it legally. And I'll step on you like an ant, Crashaw, if you keep in my way."

Frances stared at the gray-haired rancher. Her husband checked his temper, swallowing visibly. Then, he said, "You'd better leave, Wellm'n."

"You're turning me down?" Wellman looked at him coldly.

"Git out." Crashaw's voice was rising, trembling. "And, you git out, too, Tom."

Wellman spun around and started for the door. McBride stood there, savage and hopeless anger coursing through him. His father's Henry repeater, and straight-backed chair, the furniture... it was still partly his. He heard the door slam behind Wellman.

"You damn fool," he snapped. "You don't order me out of a house that's as much mine as yours."

"If it's yours, you'll fight fer it," Crashaw said.

McBride said, "Lord, man. Wellman came here to straighten things out. What's he got t' do, crawl?"

"You heard him say he wants the whole basin, Tom. You d'cide now. Fight for this spread, or git out."

"I'll be back later," McBride said. "We'll talk this out."

"Tom." His sister's voice was loud and demanding.

He turned.

"We'll talk this over now," she said bluntly.

"Look, Franny, I don't want the ranch," he said his words low, his breath siphoning out slowly.

"You walk out now, you'll never git it." She watched him, eyes flashing. Just yesterday she seemed so full of life and vigorous, sure of herself. Her life's here, he thought. Why in hell had he challenged them?

"You said you had no part in Wellm'n's business," she said.

"I don't, Franny. I didn't know it would come to this."

"You decidin' which side you're on, Tom."

"Which side . . . hell, Franny, can't you see we're all fighting the same thing."

"We're fighting Wellman."

"So," he said softly. "And, I'm his foreman. You're fighting me, too."

"You're makin' that decision, Tom?"

"Ramrodding Arrowhead's my job," he said. He hated the expression the words brought onto her face. She was his sister, so close to him; her well-being was behind his whole effort here.

"Then, it's Frank's ranch," she said. "He's

56

worked it, and he'll fight for it." And, adding as though she felt it important, "We'll fight in court, too."

He nodded and went down off the porch, untied the black and mounted.

McBride rode abreast Wellman silently, noticing the rancher sat with the hint of tension that was part of him. Susan Linford was the only hope now.

Wellman glanced angrily at him, then ahead again. "That was a damned fool idea of yours."

The foreman didn't answer.

"My crew'll just stay inside my land," the rancher went on, frowning as he groped for words. "We'll fight only when we have to."

McBride nodded and said, "I can ride to Linford's. The settlers might think different of things now."

"Damn it, I've tried hard enough." Wellman turned sharply on him, the angry color showing in his tanned, wrinkled face. "I won't go any further."

"I'll go alone."

Stubbornly, "You still want to try?"

"Yes."

The rancher slowed his gray stallion and pulled up. He sighed heavily. "I don't think it'll do any good, Tom," he said, "but you can try. I'll go into town. I was meaning to talk to Harding at the bank."

"Think it's safe?"

Wellman nodded. "No one'd bushwhack me if they see me coming from Crashaw's place."

When they reached the turn-off, McBride swung to the left, going south towards the Linford ranch.

He wished the whole thing would get cleared up, with whoever responsible for everything swinging from a rope and Crashaw and Wellman satisfied to put up their guns. Big Bend was bad enough, but what could happen would be even worse.

Ed Linford was in the meadow standing with his cattle, carbine in hand, and he turned and looked towards McBride when he broke from the woods. The short, white-haired old man walked slowly into the path leading to the house, keeping the weapon in the crook of the crippled arm as the rider approached him.

Tom McBride nodded, as though this was just a friendly visit, a casual call from a neighbor. He drew to a halt.

"You'd better turn 'round," Linford said abruptly. "You ain't wanted on this land, McBride."

"I'd like to talk to Susan."

"Bout her talkin' me out of fightin' Arrahead, I s'pose?"

"I was hoping she'd make you see how useless a range war would be."

"She tried, but the way I see it, it's stand up to Arrahead or lose your land."

"You could lose more than your land in a fight, Mister Linford."

The rancher was silent for a moment, anger still riding him, an anger that kept him scowling. Then, abruptly, he reached a decision, and straightening, said, "You ride out, McBride. I don't want to have you talkin' to my daughter, and I don't want you on my land."

McBride frowned, seeing the carbine coming up. But he had to make a last try.

"Mister Linford. The settlers've got nothing to

gain by fighting. You're wrong to lead them into..."

"They've got their land and homes, just like me. You ride out now."

Shrugging his shoulders, McBride began wheeling his horse. Susan Linford watched from the edge of the porch. He stared at her, but she gave no sign of recognition.

McBride started back along the meadow, slowing to go through the gate in the wire he hated. The tension made his nerves jump. The war's really on, he thought. I was a damn fool to think I could do anything to stop it.

SEVEN

It was more than twelve miles through hilly and rough land to Arrowhead from the Linford ranch, and McBride rode directly cross country to reach there as soon as possible. He knew Wellman would go ahead with his plans quickly; but, the big foreman hoped, if he were there, he might hold back any of the crew's rash acts.

McBride felt weariness pressing down on him as the black carried him into the Arrowhead front yard.

Ben Huntoon was at the barn, and he raised his arm hailing the rider. He crossed the yard casually, moving beside the gelding, his face serious.

"Mister Wellman back yet?" asked McBride.

Huntoon nodded. "Him and Banker Hardin' got in 'bout half hour ago," he said. He hesitated, then laughed, but the sound of it was forced. "Mebbe the boss is buyin' the bank out, too."

He was close to McBride now, and his voice suddenly became low. "Don't turn fast, Tom, but look down by the bunkhouse." His words were wound tight. "Harry Dean brought 'em back with 'im."

He turned slowly as if just looking around, and he saw the two men standing in front of the bunkhouse door. Both watched him, openly interested, the taller and thinner but leanly muscular, wore a green silk shirt with shiney buttons, either silver or pearl-plated, black Stetson and jeans. The small man's face was hostile, a stocky bantam-legged man with a mass of black wavey hair springing out where his sombrero was pushed back. There was one sameness to them, their double gunbelts and low-cut holsters thonged business-like to their thighs, branding both plainly and only as gunfighters.

"There's anotha one inside the bunkhouse same as them two," Ben said. "I don't like it, Tom."

Forcing himself to nod casually, the foreman answered, "I don't either."

Huntoon's face quivered. "I don't cotton to what the boss's goin' to use 'em for. There's lots of good folks in the Basin."

McBride's voice stayed low-pitched, but there was a definite tone to it. "I'll talk to Wellman." He swung around and strode forward towards the big house.

Looking through the window as he knocked, he saw the long living room was empty. He knocked again, then heard a door open inside. Helen Wellman crossed the room.

She pulled the door open. "Tom...Dad's been waiting for you to get back."

He stepped inside. "Ben said Mister Harding's here."

"Big transaction going on," she said, staring at him, her eyes thoughtful and troubled. "I get tired of hearing talk of nothing but money and land."

"That's what makes spreads like Arrowhead."

"I know," she said slowly, "but it can make a prison of a home, too. Land and money don't necessarily bring happiness."

She frowned, her smooth forehead becoming lined. "Dad should be more like you. Tom, I wish he didn't have that obsession for land. And I just wish the bank would stop giving him money, instead of

Mr. Harding agreeing to let him have as much as he wants."

"Anything he wants?"

"That's what they're talking about in his office," she said, her eyes showing a blend of concern and anger. "Harding's convinced Dad'll own the whole valley eventually. And he's not putting a limit on what he can borrow."

"So, that's how he's been paying such big prices," McBride said. "Harding wants to be on the right side, I guess."

"Tom," she whispered, "what's going to happen to everyone in the valley? They're good people, too good to hurt."

"No one has to sell, Helen. They..."

He broke his words off as the door to the rancher's small office opened on the right side of the room. He turned to watch Wellman and the banker come in. Behind them, Harry Dean's big form loomed in the doorway. Wellman's hard eyes stared bluntly at McBride. Harding nodded as he started past McBride. Dean moved in close behind Wellman and stood there warily watching the foreman. Something in their manner told McBride to be careful.

"You talk to the girl?" Wellman said.

McBride told him about Ed Linford stopping him, and their talk; while he spoke, the rancher frowned, his face wrinkled and dissatisfied. "I could let it ride a couple days and try again," offered McBride.

"Well, he's going to get the trouble he wants," Wellman said.

Quiet came then, with the attention centered on

Harding, a silence that stretched out until the banker, a bit uncomfortable and flustered at being drawn into the talk, took his tan Stetson from the table. "I'll go now, Lew," he said, as though he felt he was interfering with personal business. "I'll expect you in town for the money tomorrow."

"Tom, did you ever think of selling out your share of the Double F?" Wellman said. His mood was businesslike, his rough features completely unreadable.

"I've got nothing to sell out there."

"Yes, you have," Wellman said, matter-of-factly. "Harding looked up the legal stuff on your father's place. You're still as much of an owner as your sister."

"Franny owns the ranch. I gave it to her."

Coldly. "So, there's nothing binding to that." Wellman smiled slightly but it didn't change the unrevealing expression. "I'll give you five-thousand for your rights. What do you say?"

McBride felt his irritation stirring but before he could answer, Helen moved closer to her father. "You can't ask Tom to do that." She hesitated, biting her lips. "You have no right to make him sell to you."

"Get back to your room. This business has nothing to do with you."

"You said everything would be mine someday."

"And it will. Go ahead now."

"Then, this *is* my business." She stared at him guiltily, her hands clasped tightly. "Dad, we've got enough land now. We don't need the Double F, or any other place."

Wellman swore softly. "Get back into your

room." He took a step towards the girl, and she moved back, frightened, as he pointed to her bedroom.

"I'm not selling any part I own of Double F, Mister Wellman."

The rancher swung towards him. "You made up your mind about that?" He stared with wide furious eyes.

"Yes." As soon as the answer was out, McBride knew trouble was coming, knew it from the way Wellman's chin went up deliberately, and from the strained look that had come onto Harry Dean's face while the ominous silence stretched out.

"No one who works for Arrowhead says no to me," Wellman said slowly.

"It isn't mine to sell," said McBride. He knew what was coming next.

Wellman spoke quickly. "You're fired. You get out now. I'll send word into Harding and he can pay you what I owe you at the bank."

"I was going to quit, anyway," McBride said defensively. "Once I saw you were lying, I decided that."

"You saw I was lying?" Wellman's voice had a dangerous edge to it, and he inquired, "When did I lie?"

"Those hired gunslicks you've got out there," McBride said. "You said you'd give me time to try straightening things out before you brought them in. You knew Harry was going after them this morning."

The rancher exhaled deeply, seeming relieved somehow. "All right. Get out, McBride."

Harry Dean began moving at this. He left

Wellman's side and came towards McBride, his huge body bent slightly. McBride didn't move. He stood rigidly for a moment, his tall frame taut but controlled. Then, he dropped his hand down by his right side, where it hung just above his Colt. He saw Dean's hand lowering.

"Don't try it," McBride said, stepping to the right. "You aren't fast enough, Harry."

Dean stared wildly, his gun hand poised.

Wellman said, "Go ahead now, McBride. I don't want any trouble in my house."

Then, McBride looked at the rancher. "How about the ranchers? You going to make trouble for Crashaw and the rest?"

"Crashaw makes his own trouble," Wellman said.

"You going to turn those hired guns on him?"

"I told you I'd fight anyone who comes onto my land." The rancher was perfectly relaxed, sure of himself. "Now, get going before I let Harry take you on."

"You keep away from Double F," he said quietly to Wellman. "I'll see to it Crashaw doesn't come on to your land."

"Your sister gave you your choice this morning," said Wellman coldly. "Remember, you chose to go. People aren't going to listen to you, McBride."

McBride saw how they'd used him, planning it all so his trying to talk peace into Crashaw and Linford would bounce back on him. And it did. Now, his anger turned his voice to a slow dangerous monotone.

"I know Arrowhead good, Wellman," he said, a

65

confident smile touching his long, rough face. "And I know the places you've bought up. You could get back twice as much as you could give."

The rancher's face went slack. "Do all the damage you want. All's I want is land...I mean range rights, anyway."

"You just remember what I said," McBride told him. He glanced furiously at Dean.

Dean stared at him wildly. "Get goin'. Yuh heard Mistah Wellm'n say t' git out."

McBride knew he was alone now, cut off from Crashaw, Linford, his own sister, everyone of them sure where he stood by his own actions and talk. And it had all been prearranged by the man standing here watching him so contemptuously. He wondered how far Wellman would go right now. There was something pleasurable in the anger he felt. "You get me out, Harry," he said.

Dean's face was frozen, the color drained from his cheeks, leaving them white. A sneer bent his mouth as his hand opened.

"Don't be a fool! Stop that, Harry!" Wellman snapped, his voice shrill. "Get out, McBride. You won't force a fight in my house."

For some time they remained frozen in their antagonisms. Dean's hand trembled, not from fear, but from anger. Wellman's eyes never left McBride's gun. Then, McBride smiled suddenly.

He kept his hand brushing his Colt and began moving back towards the door. "You remember, Wellman," he said, "you've got a lot more to lose than I do. You keep those gunslicks on Arrowhead land, or there'll be more trouble than you can handle, I promise you that."

He stepped back through the doorway quickly,

slamming the door; then he stood quietly for a few seconds, waiting for Harry Dean to come through. There was a shuffling of feet inside, but Wellman's loud voice stopped that.

"Damn it! Hold it, Harry! You'll get your chance at him soon enough," the rancher said.

EIGHT

McBride went directly to the bunkhouse, pulled an old canvas bag from beneath his bunk, and started putting his personal belongings into it: extra clothing, some papers and books, the tintype that had hung above his bunk, not much to show for eight years' work. He'd have to get clear of the ranch fast for Dean was capable of anything, might already be planning his next tactic.

He shouldered the bag and went out to the barn. Ben Huntoon came in the back just as McBride was finishing with the girths of the double-cinched Texas saddle.

"Tom..." Huntoon breathed in deeply, catching his breath. "Yuh gotta git outa here fast. They're gonna lay fer yuh."

"Who?...slow down now."

"Harry an' a coupla the gunboys jest rode off. They're gonna lay fer yuh onna road."

"You know where?"

"No." Huntoon was calmer now.

McBride climbed onto the black, moving slowly and deliberately, a growing fear under his anger. "Tell Helen thanks for..."

Huntoon slapped the gun on his right thigh. "I'm goin' with yuh."

"No, Ben, it'll be too dangerous."

"I'm comin'," the young cowhand said, pulling his sombrero down tight over his sandy hair. "I'm leavin' anyways. I'll have a better chance gettin' out with yuh."

"Saddle up then." McBride waited, trying to figure some way out of this. And, before Huntoon came back with his roll.

"Listen to me, Ben," he said. "We can get out of this if you're willing to take a chance."

The younger man nodded.

"Once we hit the road, you'll go on alone. They aren't after you, but their attention will be on you. They'll have to keep to the woods, so I'll go along the high ground and come in from behind them. You willing to try that?"

"Sure. Look, I figger the arroyo's the best place."

"There, or near the junction. They won't do anything close enough to the ranch for anyone to hear."

They rode along the path, casually for the benefit of anyone watching from the house, and, shortly, down to the road, with McBride breaking off there and going across the flat to the distant line of willows along the creek. With the sun behind him, he had the advantage, for he could use its glare as cover when the time came. After three miles he became more tense, more cautious.

He lost sight of Huntoon, then caught him where the road ran along the wide and deep arroyo. McBride watched every tree, studying for any sign of movement, but he saw nothing. They'd have to be somewhere within the next mile, he knew. Once the road went onto the flats, they'd have no cover, because from there it was all open and straight-arrow.

Again, a quarter-mile before the junction, he lost sight of Huntoon. He'd had no right to put the boy into the tough spot. His mind roamed over his responsibility for this, then dropped all thought but on what was going on ahead.

Harry Dean and the short gunman had stopped Huntoon, and they stood in the road talking to him. McBride saw no sign of the third man.

69

He dismounted, slid his Colt from its holster, and a minute later moved through the scrub willow like a long-legged cat, making his way in a half circle, going deeper into the trees for still more cover.

Behind a ragged alder he halted. The tall gunman lounged in the corner of a growth of scrub at the road's edge, his attention on the junction, so positive was he that his prey would come that way.

"Keep your hands clear of leather," McBride said in a low voice.

The gaudily-dressed man snapped his head around, making no motion for his guns. He stiffened.

McBride gestured for him to unhook his belt. Then, when the weapons lay uselessly on the ground, "Stand up...slow now."

Moving behind his shield, McBride went onto the road.

"Get your hands up high," he called.

Harry Dean swung around, his huge body stupid with shock, the hate in his eyes changing to cold fear. The stocky gunman let out a grunt but made no movement for his weapons.

"You waiting for someone?" McBride said.

The tall gunman stared right into McBride's eyes. "We jest stopped to talk to the kid here, that's all." He was more graceful of build than McBride had first thought, in his silver-buttoned shirt, and more sure of himself.

"Yeah," Dean said, his face quivering. "Yew got no right drawin' on us fer talkin' to Benny, heah."

McBride ignored that. "Drop your guns." And to Huntoon. "You pick them up, Ben. And, get their horses back in the woods there. Get Cloud too, up..."

70

Harry Dean had made the movement he was watching for; his big body slightly bent moved ponderously as an ox towards McBride, who pivoted a step to the left, avoiding the charge and brought the barrel of his .44 crashing down. The huge man slumped into the dust.

"Get back there!" McBride snapped, jabbing the gun foreward, and the pair obeyed. Huntoon went into the woods for the horses.

McBride studied the gunmen for a few seconds. "You carry him back to Arrowhead."

"Close to ten miles back there," the tall gunman said.

The other put in, "Look here, me an' Eyster can't carry 'im that fer."

"Lift. I want to see your hands busy."

Now, the tall man named Eyster bent and took the unconscious man's legs, and the other gunman got on the arms. McBride walked a few yards behind them, his eyes sardonic and amused at their straining with their burden.

"Tell Wellman he can get your guns and mounts from the sheriff," he said finally, and he went back to where Huntoon waited with the horses.

"Wellman'll be lookin' fer us, Tom."

McBride nodded. He'd brought the young cowhand into this and now he wanted to get him out of it, at least so he wouldn't be close when Wellman tried again.

He took the three gunbelts from where Huntoon had attached them to their owners' saddle horns.

"Ben," he said, "you ride out to the Double F. Tell Frank what's happened."

"I want t' stay with you, Tom."

"No. Frank can use another gun on his spread. Besides, you'll be safer there."

71

"Look, Tom, I did good right here, didn't I."

McBride hesitated. "I'll have enough help from Bonham. You'll be in my way."

That hurt the boy. "But, I want to be in on..."

"Stay at the Double F. You'll be in on plenty before things are straightened out." He slapped Huntoon's leg. "Go ahead now."

Huntoon studied McBride thoughtfully, then pulled around and headed for the south trail. McBride lined the three horses behind the black, mounted and continued on towards Cavanagh.

Forty-five minutes later he entered Grant Street and went slowly to the jail, aware of the grim faces that watched his progress through the town.

McBride dismounted at the hitchrail between the bank and the jail.

Sheriff Matt Bonham was sitting at the rolltop desk in his office. He swung around in the battered swivel chair and faced McBride as he came through the door. Old Pop Holmes looked up from his whittling, his wrinkled face interested.

Bonham sounded a bit surprised. "Didn't 'spect you in town for quite 'while, Tom."

McBride walked to the desk and laid down the gunbelts. "I took these from Harry Dean and two hired guns Wellman got in. I told them you'd give them back." He motioned to the door. "Their horses are outside."

"Have some trouble?" In the darkening office, McBride could see Bonham's thin face was hard and cautious.

"That's right. I quit Wellman today. He sent Dean and his playmates out to give me a lesson." He didn't like the way the sheriff seemed to be

72

silently appraising his words. "I was wrong about Wellman, Matt. He *is* out for trouble."

Bonham nodded. "Banker Hardin' said Wellm'n was goin' t'fire you. He said Wellm'n suspected you of havin' somethin' t' do with the trouble in the Basin."

"His bank'll gain from Wellman's winning out. You can see that, Matt."

"You took these from Dean and two gunslicks, eh?" he said, rubbing his cheek absently.

"Yes, Ben Huntoon helped me."

"Oh, yeah. Hardin' said Wellm'n thought Ben was in on the trouble, too."

"Ben?"

"Yeah. He said Wellm'n'd fire him, too."

Bonham was silent. "You know Banker Hardin's straight on this, Tom," he said shortly. "He's just a businessman in this. So why should he lie?"

A flush came onto McBride's face. "What are you driving at?"

"There's no reason for a bank president to back up Wellm'n. His bank deals with everyone in the Basin."

"He's smart enough to get on the strong side."

"Listen here, Tom," Bonham said angrily, "you're in trouble, and you want me t' pull you out. If you're tellin' the truth, why don't you go to Crashaw? He's your folk."

"All right," McBride said, holding back his anger, "I'll go it alone."

"You can't go it 'lone," Bonham said. "An' any trouble's my business. But, I'm not sure about you, Tom. You might as well know that."

"I said I'd go it alone."

"If you did take those guns away like y' said, you'll be havin' people lookin' fer you. Harry Dean'll not stop til' he's had his way. An', I don't want no one hurt in my town. You hear that, Tom?"

"I was planning to take a room at the hotel."

"No. Dundee'll let you use his back room. Lock the door to the saloon. Me and Loomis'll keep an eye on the ends of the alley."

"Thanks, Matt."

McBride went outside and along the walk to Dundee's, keeping well in the shadows thrown by the false fronts of the buildings. Why should Bonham get so one-way? Had Wellman planned everything so well that even the law was convinced he was in some way responsible for Alf Paulson and the rest? He'd better be especially careful or someone in town here might try to do the job before Wellman got to him.

The freshening evening wind was already cooling the air, making him feel more comfortable as he knocked on the back door.

Dundee's Sioux handyman opened the door. "Tell Will I want to see him," said McBride.

The Indian nodded, watching closely, and McBride sensed the fear that was in him, so he looked away, towards the end of the alley. Two faces watched him. Unconsciously, his hand went to his six-gun, and the inquisitive faces pulled back from sight and behind cover.

They'll know where to look, he thought. Well, damn it, he had a better chance this way.

Will Dundee's fat body came into the doorway. "Git the hell outa the alley, Tom," he said. "You c'n end things up quick like that."

McBride asked him about the room.

"Sure," Dundee grunted, and stepped back to let him in. He pointed to some tables he used when the bar got crowded, "Pile 'em 'gainst the inside door. Them tops are thick."

"I'll do that."

Dundee handed him a key. "Keep it locked from the inside."

"I'll bring in something to eat later, Tom. Good luck."

The night coolness outside failed to penetrate into the room, and McBride felt the sticky sweat all over him. He ate little of the meal Will Dundee brought back, but drank both bottles of the cold beer. And he waited, because that was all he could do.

He dozed and woke. McBride leaned with his back to the thick-topped tables piled against the door, feeling the desperation of a cornered man. The hours passed that way.

A pounding behind him shocked him out of a half-sleep. He swung around, gun in hand.

"Tom! Tom! Open up!"

The knocking sounded again, more insistant, and now he recognized the voice as Ben Huntoon's.

He pushed the tables aside and pulled the door back, still keeping his body out of the opening, just in case.

Huntoon stepped into the room, his eyes staring. "Tom. Where in hell are yuh?" Will Dundee was behind him.

"Right here, Ben." He saw Huntoon's expression then and felt the sudden cold shock that tense anticipation brings. "What is it, Ben . . . they get Franny or Frank?"

The boy shook his head. "It was Ed Linford's place they hit. They killed the old man."

NINE

People begun crowding into the big saloon, and for an instant McBride studied the faces intently, suddenly realizing the killing could be part of a plan to get him out in the open.

"They get the girl, too, Ben?" he asked.

"No. She was inside the house," Huntoon's loud voice said. "She's sent one o' the settlers t' Double F, an' Cranshaw tol' me t' git the sheriff."

McBride put on his sombrero and left the saloon. After an hour, Ben and he had reached Linford's ranch. He cursed his own stupidity. This was something he should have expected and warned about. Wellman had said Linford would get the trouble he was looking for.

This time there were more settlers, and some women mixed into the crowd. McBride left his horse near the well and walked to the house. Men talking in low voices near one of the timbers supporting the porch turned to look at him. He saw Evans and Barstow in the group.

Sheriff Bonham was standing at the further end of the porch. A settler beside him spoke, and the little lawman turned, his cautious face hard and lined in the morning shadows.

McBride said, "You got any idea who did it, Matt?"

Bonham hesitated, shaking his head slowly. "We had tracks as far as the road, but lost 'em."

"How many of them were there?"

"Only one," Bonham said, nothing showing on his face. "I'm glad you were inside Dundee's, Tom. The girl saw 'im. Said he was tall and rode a black like yours."

McBride glanced around at the watching groups and saw their stares, reading the open hostility in the uncertain light.

"They wanted to ride out t' Arrowhead," Bonham said. They're mad, Tom, so you be damned careful."

"Didn't you tell them I was in town?"

"Some of 'em don't care. You fit the description, that's enough."

"Where's the girl?"

"Inside. She's takin' it pretty hard."

McBride turned and walked back to the door, his boots knocking loudly in the potent silence. He went around the group of men that wouldn't open up so he could pass. Someone shouted an oath at him, but he paid no attention.

He opened the door and went inside. Franny was there, sitting with three settler women. Susan was not there. Linford's body was laid out on the couch, a blanket under him and a clean white sheet covering the whole corpse. The scene seemed out of place in the neatly-furnished and pleasant room.

McBride stared at the covered body for a few moments, his face hard and concerned. Here was the settler who'd beaten the land and had become a rancher, McBride thought, who fought like an unbroken stallion at Big Bend, and who'd brought the ranchers and settlers together. A good man, who'd been part of the promise of the land.

A movement behind him made him turn, and McBride saw that Franny had stood and was coming towards him.

She stopped, close to him. "Susan thought it was you," she said quietly, "'til the sheriff said you were in town."

He looked down at the body and then back to

77

her. "She thought I'd do that," he said, his voice tight. He stood there for a few seconds, staring at the closed kitchen door. "What'll she do now?"

"Frank and I want her to come to our place."

Looking at his sister quickly, "I didn't see Frank outside."

"He's at the ranch," she told him softly. "He was afraid they might try burnin' us out."

"Well, I tried to warn you," McBride said, shaking his head, "but Frank wouldn't listen. Linford either."

Her hand gripped his arm. "You knew this was goin' t' happen?"

Irritation mixed in with his sorrow. "I told Frank that Wellman would get tough."

"Did you know they were comin' after Ed?" Her voice was low, a bit horror-struck. "Did you know that?"

"I knew they'd start with someone. I sent Ben to Double F because I thought you'd be hit first."

"I'm glad it wasn't your fault," she said, the words barely audible.

The kitchen door opened and Susan came into the room. She stopped, standing there stiffly when she saw him.

He said awkwardly, hesitantly, "I'm sorry, Susan."

She bit her lip, her white face composed. "Why? You knew it would happen. Only there's no body tied down over a saddle this time."

McBride followed, closing the door behind him. He didn't care what the others thought, but it was important that she understand. She sat down at the table and looked at him.

"I thought it was you," she said, and there was a

sudden trembling anger in her voice. Her body was rigid. "The rider yelled into the house for us. It sounded like your voice. My father went out because he knew you wouldn't shoot." It was a struggle, but she controlled her voice.

"Susan, I was in town."

"Sheriff Bonham told me."

"Did you see the killer?"

"Enough of him to see he was tall and riding a black gelding." Suddenly she turned her face away from him, her shoulders shaking. "You get out of here. I don't want you on my land. If you hadn't come around here all those times, my father would never have gone out on that porch alone."

He looked down at the slight figure in the chair, wishing he could reach her. It was useless to try to argue, for her mind was made up, and she would see only what she wanted.

"Listen to me," he said sharply. "I know everyone at Arrowhead. Maybe the killer sat his saddle a certain way." He was thinking of Harry Dean, now. "Did he lean forward over the horn like he was tired?"

Susan shook her thin shoulders. "He sat straight. I could see that, but he kept his face turned away from the light."

"Tell the whole thing from the beginning. You were sleeping when someone yelled into the house. Right?"

Standing, she pointed to the kitchen lamp. "I had that in the bedroom," she said. "And, when my father went outside, I stayed in the doorway so he could see out on the porch. They talked for a little while. The only thing I heard was something the rider said about selling our land. I could hear

79

my father saying no." She went on. "It happened so fast. They were talking like that and then the shooting started. He only shot three times. My father didn't make a sound. He just fell."

Now, she was crying again. "You didn't see his face?"

She shook her head. "I just thought it was you."

"Why me?"

"You've been here so often. I thought you were trying again."

"In the middle of the night?"

Susan shrugged her shoulders, but it wasn't an indifferent shrug. "I don't know...maybe it was the white buttons on your shirt. I could see..."

She nodded to his own shirt. "I could see them in the little light there was. I remembered you had..."

McBride's eyes reflected sudden awareness. His voice was sure. "Could the shirt have been green instead of blue?"

"It was too dark. But it looked blue." She was silent a moment. "It could've been any dark color."

His mouth cracked at the edges, but not in a smile. "I'll bring in someone for you to see. Maybe you'll recognize him."

"You think you know who did it?"

"Wellman hired a gunslick who wears silver buttons," he said coldly. "I'll bring him to Double F for you to see."

"I'll be right here, if you bring anyone in."

He frowned. "You can't stay here. Franny and Frank said they'd take you in. You go there."

"I'm staying here. I worked this ranch with my father. I can ride, rope and herd cattle. And use a gun if I have to. Wellman did this so I'd sell. Well, I'm not selling."

Linford's death was a warning to the settlers to break off with the ranchers, McBride knew. Susan's refusal to sell would keep that obstacle in front of Wellman. They'll kill her, too, he thought.

"You can't stay here alone, Susan."

"I can," she snapped. "I have to."

"They'll come back," he said slowly. "They'll kill your cattle, wreck your fences and burn your buildings. Wellman'll get this place for taxes then. You're out of your mind to stay here."

She looked at his frown. "Then, I'm out of my mind. But I won't go out after dark. I'll shoot anyone who rides in here at night."

"How about having Ben Huntoon work here? He could sleep in the barn."

"No, I'll stay alone."

He went out and around the corner of the house to the porch. Sheriff Bonham was standing near the door.

"Arrahead did a damn good job heah," a lanky young dungareed settler called.

McBride looked around, seeing the troublesome settler close behind him. The youngster looked wild, his thick neck and jowls red with emotion. McBride's fists tightened, coming up quickly, but not fast enough. The boy's right swung out, catching him off balance, the long vicious hook pounding into his chest and spinning him around so he crashed against one of the square timber roof supports. McBride doubled, then straightened, his lips tight.

Bonham shouted, "That's enough." He grabbed

McBride's shoulder roughly, pulled him back, and stood between him and the crowd.

The young settler hesitated, throwing a glance around to see if he had any backing. The approaching men were loud, making no secret of the fact their sympathies were not with McBride. Encouraged, the settler snapped, "'Bout time we really started on Arrahead."

"Yeah," the cowhand named Evans yelled. "We'll get McBride outa this rite now."

The small sheriff took a step towards the crowd. "McBride was in Cavanagh all night. He didn't have nothin' to do with this." He said over his shoulder to McBride, "You git your horse, Tom. I'll be 'long in a minute."

McBride moved backwards and stepped down from the porch. He went slowly to his black and mounted. Soon Bonham left the porch, climbed onto his horse, and rode to McBride's side.

"You'd better be more careful, Tom. Some of 'em have the idea you put on an act in town to keep me there all night."

That shocked McBride. "They think I'm still with Arrowhead?"

Bonham nodded. "They're gittin' harder t' handle, Tom. They could do somethin' violent before long."

"You'd better stay in town," Bonham said. "Either me or Pat'll keep close for 'while."

"I will, but I've got to go out to Arrowhead first."

The sheriff stared at him. "Alone?"

McBride told him what Susan had said about the buttons on the killer's shirt. "One of those gunslicks named Eyester was tall and had silver buttons." His voice was quiet, firm. "I figure I know Arrowhead well enough to get in and bring him back."

"You sure he's the man?"

"No. But if Susan could identify him, it'd be the start of cleaning things up."

Bonham thought about that. "I'll ride out with you," he said. "I'd like t' git a look at jest what Wellman's linin' up out theah, anyways."

TEN

It was after eight when they went onto Arrowhead land. They came in from the front of the big ranch house, trotting up the long, tree-lined drive to the veranda. Carl Dawson, one arm in a sling, stood watching them from the corner of the house, a tense, unnatural smile on his lips, as if he wanted to say something.

Helen Wellman looked out the window at them, then stepped onto the veranda. She was clearly startled at seeing McBride.

Bonham said, "I want t' see your father."

Her worried look shifted to McBride. "What happened, Tom?"

"There's been another killing."

"Nate Antrim?" Her voice was cold, controlled.

"No, Ed Linford. The settler who bought the Crockett place last year."

Four men, he noticed, now stood with Dawson. Looking beyond them he could see the stocky, bantam-legged gunman standing in the open barn door. He alone was armed, his hands close to his guns, and the same hostility and hate still apparent in his stare. McBride turned back to the veranda when he heard the front door open.

Wellman walked out, followed by Henry Dean who wore a wide bandage circling his head, covering his torn scalp.

"More trouble, Matt?" Wellman said, frowning.

"Linford was shot and killed this mornin'." Bonham looked bluntly at him, his eyes narrow and penetrating. "We think mebbe one of your men did it."

Wellman's face reddened. "Well, you look them over, Matt." He nodded towards the watching group. "Talk to them."

Bonham smiled coldly. "This gunboy's named Eyester. He's tall and wears a green shirt with silver buttons."

"Oh, that one. I fired him." He looked at McBride and added in a surprisingly gentle voice, "I hired him to handle troublemakers like McBride, here, but when I found out he couldn't, I let him go."

Helen said, "But he was here last night, Dad."

The silence stretched out as Wellman looked at her, a faint warning in his hard eyes and deliberate manner. "He left after that, Helen. You saw him go."

"Yes, he left before sunset," she murmured, as though she had suddenly remembered.

McBride motioned towards the barn and said softly, "How about the little rooster down there? He and Eyester were riding together?"

"I decided to keep him on."

"You don't know where Eyester is?" Bonham said.

"Listen to me!" Wellman's voice was high but controlled. "I don't know who killed Linford. I've hired some guns, but it's only to defend what's mine. And they have orders to shoot any trespasser. But, I'll fight only when someone gives me trouble on my own property. Do you understand that?"

"I'm goin' after Eyester, Lew," the sheriff said, "an' I don' want any of your hands shootin' at me."

"They won't." Wellman looked at McBride resentfully, as if he blamed him for putting him into this position. "You'd better check on where McBride was during the shooting."

"I know where he was."

"Well, my guess is that someone took the trouble as an excuse to get rid of Linford."

"You see it that way, huh?"

"I know none of my crew did it, Matt."

The sheriff began moving towards his horse, an enigmatic expression on his face. "I hope you weren't in on it, Lew," he said. "I'm goin' t' get Eyester."

"You can use some of my crew. As many as you want."

"No. I've got all the help I need.

"Well, remember I offered."

Bonham frowned. "I will," he said, glancing at the Arrowhead crew. He studied the men for a moment in silence. Shortly, "I don't want to see that gunboy in town, Lew."

"He works for me," Wellman said, the words falling out quickly. Harry Dean stepped down onto the top step. He glowered like a wrestler ready to rush out of his corner, keeping an eye on the sheriff, but his glare was all for McBride.

"You listen t' me," Bonham said, his voice tight and dangerous. "You hire guns to protect your prop'ty, it's one thing. But you keep them rite here on your prop'ty." His eyes swung over to Dean. "I don't want anyone who thongs his gun down in my town. Is that clear?"

Finally, Wellman said, "All right. Young doesn't go into town. But you'd better pass the word about trespassing on my ranch...that goes for any land I buy up, too."

Bonham nodded and swung his mount around.

McBride followed, pulling up abreast once they were back on the drive.

"You go on back t' town," he said to McBride, his calm face revealing no trace of his thoughts.

"I don't think it's safe to go riding alone through these hills, Matt."

"There's no danger, for me at least," Bonham said, a solemn line about his cautious mouth. "Last thing Wellman'd want is me bein' found dead rite after leavin' his spread."

McBride was silent, studying the small man with a little frown. "You figure Wellman's gunslick is still around?"

"I'm goin' t' have a look-see, anyways. So you git on back t' town."

Touching the black with his spurs, McBride started him off, opening the horse up and letting him run hard until he was safely past the junction and out on the flat. There he stopped to let the animal blow, sitting his saddle easily while he built a smoke.

He was licking the cigarette into shape when he heard the heavy clop-clopping of a horse coming fast on the hard-pack behind him. He sat, nervous and uncertain with his hand on his Colt, watching the spot where the road left the woods, the dry taste of fear in his mouth, ready to shoot and run if it was trouble.

Shortly, Helen Wellman came into view, riding side-saddle on a white-footed mare. The bright morning sunlight glinted on her ruffled hair and smooth light skin. She was almost to him when he saw the coagulated blood at the corner of her mouth and dark bruise running along the right jawbone.

She drew the horse to a halt, and, abruptly, "Where's the sheriff?"

"He's looking for Eyester back on Arrowhead."

For a few moments she hesitated. "Dad hit me, Tom," she told him in a small, still amazed voice, her eyes beginning to fill. "I've done the best I could. Everything I've done was to keep his home like he wanted it. He's yelled before, but he's never hit me before." She shivered and ran her hand across her mouth. "I want the sheriff to keep him from taking me back there. I won't go back there."

"What reason did he have to do a thing like that!"

The girl shook her head quickly. "There was no reason for it. No reason for hitting me."

"Helen, did you do something...say something?" She seemed unsteady, and he took her right arm and held it.

She sighed. "He's been shouting at me everytime I open my mouth lately. I don't do anything right. You've been in the house. You've heard him."

"Was it because you said Eyester didn't leave until late last night? Was it that?"

"No. Eyester did leave late," she answered, straightening. "He was telling the truth. I just said I was glad it wasn't Nate Antrim who'd been killed, and he got mad."

"Nate?" His hand tightened on her arm. "Why'd you figure it'd be Nate?"

"When he quit, Dad was yelling at him." She stared fearfully at him, held by his hard eyes. "Dad was warning him about something. And he threatened to have him killed."

"Why?"

"I don't know. I'm just glad it wasn't Nate. Do you know where he is, Tom?"

"No." He remembered how Antrim had left the ranchhouse looking at no one, saying nothing and getting his belongings together hurriedly. Why would Wellman threaten him, McBride wondered. Why Antrim? There had to be something important there if Wellman reacted so violently at her mentioning it.

"Where can I go?" she said. "He'll be coming after me."

"All right. Pat Loomis can take care of you until Bonham gets back."

"Dad would get me out of the jail, somehow." She was silent, thinking. At least she asked quietly, "Do you think Franny would take me in at the Double F, Tom?"

He shook his head quickly. "I can't ask her or Frank. You father found out, he'd have a good reason to shoot the place up."

"But I've got to go somewhere he doesn't suspect," she said indignantly, but catching herself she watched him closely.

McBride saw something in her expression then, a trace of the demanding arrogance of Lew Wellman, and the unexpected discovery made him wonder about her.

"Take me anywhere, Tom. Just until Bonham gets back."

"Turn your horse around," he said.

She shook her head quickly, her mouth shaking. "I won't go back to Arrowhead." Her fear was shifting to anger. "I'll wait here on the trail for the sheriff. I can hide if..."

He took hold of her bridle and began turning her

mare. "You do what I tell you," he said. "They'll never think of looking at Linford's place. We'll see if Susan will take you in."

Her face brightened. "Oh, thank you, Tom," she said, and she rode back towards the junction with him.

McBride wasn't sure just how good the idea was. Susan was under an emotional stress and he wasn't sure she'd stand for anything like this. When they reached the gate in the Linford fence, he said to Helen, "You let me do all the talking. She's had a hard time of it, so don't interrupt, no matter what she says."

The front door opened when they went into the meadow and Susan came onto the porch, wearing faded jeans and shirt and holding a rifle pointed at them.

"Don't get down," Susan said. "You're going right back out, McBride."

"I want you to let Helen stay here a while."

Susan's lips tightened. "What?" she said, glancing towards Helen. Her eyes rested on the bruised jaw and lip.

"Her father beat her. Keep her here until Matt Bonham gets back to town."

There was a quizzical, almost an amused look in Susan's face while she hesitated, deciding. McBride moved in the saddle, nervously. He wanted to get this straightened out and find Nate Antrim. He might have some information he could use.

"All right," Susan said finally, "she can stay here." And, when McBride began dismounting, "Not you...you get out."

Susan stepped back to let Helen go inside the

90

house. She was silently staring at the daughter of the man whom she felt had been responsible for her father's death. McBride sensed the tension gripping the small girl, understanding it.

He leaned forward. "Watch Helen. You can't be too sure."

Susan stared wide-eyed. "You think she could be lying?"

"I don't know. But she's still Wellman's daughter. So you be careful," he said seriously. Then, he reined the black around and started across the meadow.

ELEVEN

McBride walked down the dusty length of Grant Street just after three that afternoon. He'd tried the hotel and Mae Mullin's boarding house. There were similar answers at both places: they hadn't seen Nate Antrim during the last two days; and Harry Dean had been in about noon looking for Antrim, too. Wellman was afraid of something, McBride knew. He wouldn't send Dean out looking in the open like that if he wasn't more concerned about what Antrim knew than he was about keeping up his pretence of innocence.

McBride pushed through Dundee's double doors, welcoming the dark coolness of the saloon. Men at the bar and tables watched him, slowing their talk to an awkward silence. Dundee was behind the bar and he came to where McBride stopped.

"Heard yuh got through at Arrowhead." The fat saloon-keeper spoke more loudly than usual as he wiped the bar.

Tom McBride frowned at the obviousness of the remark. He nodded. "Will, have you seen Nate Antrim around since yesterday?" he said, his hard face unchanged, revealing nothing.

Dundee turned his bulky body and took a bottle from the top shelf. "Harry Dean was in lookin' for him this mornin'," he said, a solemn line about his wide mouth.

"We're looking for different reasons, Will."

McBride saw that the onlookers were catching every word, and thinking one of them might know where Antrim was, he glanced around at them quizzically. For a few moments, the men stared back in silence, and he knew they still didn't trust him. He turned back to the drink Dundee had poured him.

"Well, have you seen Nate, Will?" he said. "You'll do him a favor if you tell me."

"Harry's out gunnin', huh?"

"Not sure. But, I'm not. That's what you're wondering about, isn't it?"

Will Dundee was silent, watching McBride down his whiskey. Finally, he said, "Nate hasn't been in today, Tom."

McBride took out a silver dollar and placed it on the bar, nodding for a refill. "If you know where he is," he said, "let me know. I don't want to take a chance on Nate's getting shot at."

Dundee said quickly, "You don't know 'bout Barstow, huh, Tom?"

"What about him?"

"He got shot at this mornin'. He was workin' out 'hind his barn when someone shot from the trees out there. Bullet just missed his head."

"Damn good shootin'," someone said. "Them tree's so close a man could only miss if he had a mind to."

"So, Barstow's sellin' out," Dundee said. "He figgers mebbe it was a warnin'. He don't want t'take chances with his woman and kids."

That was how they'd do it with Barstow, McBride thought. The little rancher was known as a shrewd but honest man who played everything safe. There was a significance to this: Wellman knew he could drive men like Barstow out anytime, so getting after them now meant he was rushing up things. "Anyone try to talk him into staying?"

Dundee smiled crookedly. "There was talk 'bout gettin' a U.S. marshal in, but he wouldn't listen."

McBride held his glass in his hand, turning it and studying the amber liquid. He finished it and began moving towards the door.

"Wait a minute," Dundee said. He had come to the end of the bar and was nervously mopping an imaginary wet spot on the counter. "I've got some o' your roll in the back room. You want it?"

He hadn't left anything here, McBride knew. He faced the fat man and saw his solemn expression. The onlookers were watching; what Dundee was pulling wasn't fooling them.

"Sure, I'll take it now," McBride said, shrugging. He followed into the storeroom.

The saloonkeeper turned quickly, his face grim. "Nate gets killed, they'll blame you," he said.

"Then, you know where he is."

Closing the door, "He's at my house. He's scared, Tom. He won't come out, even for meals."

McBride stared at him, slightly surprised. The last thing he'd expected was that the Dundees would stick their necks out. "You're all right, Will. Be damn careful, though."

"Dean never figgered on me," Dundee said, smiling, a bit proud. "I don't like people bein' pushed 'round. Anyways, they'd be bound to be a day they'd start on me."

"I'll go out this way," said McBride. He started for the back door. "Look, keep everyone inside here. I don't want anyone seeing me going into your place."

"You tell Annie I sed it was all right," Dundee told him, and McBride saw deep concern on the wide, swollen face.

Three minutes later McBride came to the small

backyard of Dundee's home. He opened the gate in the white picket fence and went hurriedly to the door.

Stepping into the kitchen as soon as Annie Dundee opened the door, he told her what her husband had said. She was small and thin, an odd contrast to Dundee; but where McBride was concerned, she was as trusting.

"I'll call Nate," she said.

"No. I'll go up."

"Be sure you let him know it's you, Tom."

He knocked on the door, "Nate...hey, Nate, it's Tom McBride."

The bed creaked and boots skuffed on the floor, but there was no other sound.

"It's Tom McBride. Let me in, Nate."

"You 'lone, Tom?"

"Yes. Let me in."

After a moment of silence, "You walk in with yuh hans up, Tom. You be sure theah up."

"Sure." McBride raised his hands over his head.

The door opened quickly. Antrim was standing to the right side of the doorway holding his six-gun. It surprised McBride to see how bad he looked. He wore work clothes, his dark face a stubble of beard. His mustache was scraggy and hair mussed, and big pouches lined his tight face beneath bloodshot eyes.

"Step in, Tom, and undo yuh belt."

"Hell, I'm here to help, Nate," McBride said, slightly puzzled and angry.

Antrim rubbed his knotted forehead. "Off with the gun, I sed."

McBride loosened the belt and tossed it onto the bed. "You're in a bad way, Nate."

"You know theah lookin' fer me."

"I got through at Arrowhead, too," McBride told him.

Suddenly Antrim stepped back to the window where he could look down at the street. "Wheah's yuh horse?" he asked.

"At the hotel. I looked everywhere for you. Finally, Will told me you were here."

"He did, huh?" Antrim looked back at McBride now, seeming to be more sure of himself. "Why'd Wellman send Dean aftah me?"

"I was going to ask you that."

Antrim said angrily, "They got no right keepin' aftah me. I got my pay and roll. They got no claim on me."

"You know why they're after you?"

"No." Antrim looked away from McBride's eyes, biting his lip.

"Damn it, you do know. Why, Nate?"

"They got no real reason. They shouldn't worry 'bout me."

"Why should they think they've got to worry?"

"They've got no reason, I tell yuh."

"Listen," McBride said, a flush of anger coming onto his face. "You hold something in, they'll have reason to hunt you down. You tell me, they won't have any reason to..."

"I tol' Wellman I di'n't heah nothin'."

"When didn't you hear anything?"

"When I went up to git my pay. I walked in while they wuz talkin'."

"Look, Nate. Will and his wife are sticking their necks out for you. And you won't talk up. What the hell you want to do, get them killed, too?"

96

Again, Antrim searched McBride, as if determining how deeply his thoughts went. His face changed; it sagged wearily. "Theah usin' Kingman's old line camp neah the pass, I think. Dean was askin' if he should go out theah when I came in."

He leveled his Colt again when McBride reached for his gun. McBride took the belt and held it on his hand as he went for the door. Antrim followed him, grabbing the big man's shoulder.

"You don' blame me, Tom? You know theah out aftah me?"

"You'd better stay here until Bonham comes up," McBride said, impatiently pulling his shoulder free.

"Nothin' else I could do. I hadta keep shut." Nervously, he tugged at his chin. "Wellman h'ain't stopped at nothin'. You know that, Tom."

McBride didn't say anything. He closed the door behind him, hesitating only to buckle on the belt, glad to be away from looking at what it all had done to the cowhand.

He went along the street, followed by dozens of eyes, directly to the jail. Pat Loomis moved out of the doorway to let him in, and McBride followed him across the plank floor.

"Where's Matt?" asked McBride.

"Last thing anyone saw of him, he was ridin' with you," the stringy deputy said.

Silently, McBride studied Loomis with a little frown. "I left him out to Arrowhead. He wanted to look the place over."

"Barstow was sniped at this mornin'," Loomis

said. "Seems like you've been takin' up most of Matt's time when things like that happen. You see what it looks like?"

McBride waited.

"Matt and me stayed in town waitin' for someone to come after you in Dundee's," Loomis said, rubbing his long face. "And now Matt's out ridin' with you when Barstow's shot at." He stared McBride right in the eyes. "That don't look so good for you."

"It still doesn't point to me," McBride said sharply. "You knew where I was all the time."

Loomis was quiet for a moment, looking up at the wanted posters. McBride broke the silence.

"I think I've got something," he said. "Nate Antrim told me they're using Kingman's old line camp."

The deputy frowned. "People've been lookin' fer Nate. Just an hour 'go Harding wanted me to get him. Sed to let him know as soon as I found him."

Now Hardin's in on it, too, McBride thought. Why should he get in on the hunt? Harding worked only for his own interests; he was notorious for doing nothing unless there was a profit in it for him. But, there was no profit in Antrim. "He tell you why he wanted Nate?" he asked.

"Yeah. He's got his pay at the bank."

McBride nodded coldly. "Antrim said he had his pay. So, don't tell Harding he's in town."

"What about Antrim?" Loomis said. "Don't you think word'll get back to Wellman he's still in town?"

For a moment McBride thought about that. "I'm going out to the linecamp," he said finally. "Will you come out when Matt gets back?"

"Not unless he sends me. Too damn many things happen when one of us is out with you."

"You know who's to blame, Loomis: Wellman, Dean, those hired guns. But they can't be touched until it's proven. I've probably got the best lead yet, and all you do is sit on your tail."

"Wal, I'm doin' what I think right." Loomis's voice was sincere, his eyes tight and unfriendly.

McBride shrugged his shoulders. "I know that, Pat," he said, smiling sardonically.

He went out, stepping down into the street from the boardwalk, and walked towards his gelding in front of the hotel.

TWELVE

McBride followed the road coming from the pass for more than an hour, then reined south along the plain trail leading to Sun Dance Canyon, taking care to check for anyone following him. Forty minutes later, he turned the black east again to approach the line camp from the wooded rear.

The sun was still more than an hour above the horizon when he sighted the small corral and buildings. He edged his mount slowly closer to the clearing, stopping shortly behind cover of some scrub. There were two horses tethered to the fence of the little corral, another near an ancient barn that sagged as though a good wind would finish it; but, he saw no other movement there or at the single-room wooden shack.

For three minutes he sat, watching debating his next move. He took his Winchester from the scabbard and began to dismount.

"Jest put that theah gun back where you got it." The voice came from his left, the words slow and distinct. And when McBride obeyed, "Move out in the open, now!"

McBride nudged the black through the scrub and turned to the left. Chink Miller stepped out from behind a tall willow.

"Wal, I'll be damned." The cowhand's solemn face broke into a smile. "You can git shot comin' up like thet, Tom." He lowered his carbine.

"Glad you waited before you shot, Chink," he said bluntly.

"Boss Wellman doesn't want any shootin' now, Tom. Miss Helen's missin', and he's called

everythin' off for 'while. But you'd better git ridin'.
Young's down at the shack."

"Eyester there, Chink?"

Miller stared at him. "Hell, no. Fact is, we're
burnin' the place down so..."

From in front of the small shack, Young called
in a high, demanding voice, "Who in hell's thet,
Miller? Bring 'im down heah."

"You'd better go down," said Miller, his face
solemn again.

The slight pressure of McBride's knees started
the black forward. Brazos had stepped out of the
barn and watched him come across the clearing.
The short, bantam-legged gunman adjusted his
belt, raising the weapons at his hips a trifle. The
air smelled heavily of lamp oil.

Young studied McBride, his lips twitching into a
wry smile. "What yuh want, Jasper?" he asked
irritably.

"Eyester. I figured he was using his place."

"Wal, yuh've seen he ain't, Jasper," he said.
"Yuh c'n see we're burnin' this place. Boss thinks
mebbe if Crashaw set a fire here, it'd burn that
good timber back theah." Young motioned towards the direction of the road. "Yew ride out now.
Figger you're lucky the boss called off the shootin'
fer 'while."

"Mind if I take a look inside?"

"Ride out, I said." Young gestured impatiently
again. "You get me riled, Jasper, I'll forget what
the boss said 'bout wantin' things peaceful. So yew
fergit Bob Eyester. Git out now, Jasper!"

McBride stared as the short gunman stepped
back, moving quickly out of his way to allow him to
turn his mount. Young was simply following

orders, letting him go like this, and McBride could see he didn't like it. He lived by his guns, was kept alive by them. McBride shrugged and began reining around.

Brazos called, "Hey, Young, wanna look in this barn? See if I poured the oil right?"

"Yuh make sure McBride goes," Young said to Miller, then turned and sauntered towards the barn.

"Better go, Tom," said Miller. "He's a bad one to cross."

Nodding, McBride swung the black around wide, moving off past the shack. He kept the animal close to the building, leaning his long body forward as he passed a window. There was plates on the table, water in the jug, and one bunk had been pulled away from the wall so it'd face the door.

The word had gotten back to Wellman that he was looking for Antrim, and the rancher wasn't taking any chances.

"What in hell yuh doin'?" Young's voice was loud and cold. He had come out of the barn and watched from where the horses were racked at the corral. He mounted the gray stallion and quickly crossed the yard towards McBride. "I told yuh to git out, Jasper," he said, his flat eyes irritable. "Yuh had to have one look, huh?"

"I was leaving," McBride said.

"Yuh got me mad, Jasper," Young said, gesturing angrily, the fury straining his wide face. "Yuh go 'head and do what yuh want like yuh're talkin' to one of these dumb cowhands." He straightened abruptly, the short rein on his temper broken, his right hand falling towards his gun.

McBride moved then, jabbing his knees hard

into the black. The sudden pressure sent the gelding lunging forward, crashing into Young's mount. McBride's outstretched hand knocked Young's gun-hand down, his right smashing savagely into the stocky man's face. Thrown off balance like that, the gunman bent forward quickly to keep his saddle, moving directly into another pounding blow. Dazed, he held on tightly to keep his saddle.

McBride's hand snapped down and came up with his Colt. He backed his horse slowly, holding his .44 aimed at the gunman's chest.

"Don't try drawing," he said coldly. His glance missed no movement on the part of Brazos and Miller, too.

There was a thin trickle of blood at Young's nose. He ran the back of one hairy hand across his lip, smearing the red. "I'll get yuh..." he shouted.

The six-gun in McBride's hand moved out a bit more. "You've said enough," he told him quietly. "Drop them guns now!"

Young went silent, an involuntary look of fear coming into his eyes. The knowledge that his life would end here and now gripped him, holding him taut for a moment. Then he unbuckled his gunbelt.

"Give it here," McBride said. He eyed the other Arrowhead riders cautiously, seeing no sign of anger on their faces. "I don't want him borrowing your guns," he said.

"He won't," Miller said, and Brazos nodded.

McBride knew Young wouldn't come after him with two unwilling witnesses there. "I'll leave your guns on the trail," he said.

"Wellman's orders'll be off soon, McBride," Young said. "I'm comin' after yuh first."

"Then, you'd better be more careful," said

McBride. He nudged the black into motion and went along the trail going out to the road, turning in the saddle to watch Young, who still stared after him, his eyes tight and cold.

Once out of sight, McBride spurred his mount, opening him up and letting him run. He headed for the jail, noticing that more people than usual were about the porches and walks. When he was passing Dundee's the batwings swung open and the fat saloonkeeper came down the steps towards the black.

Dundee motioned anxiously for McBride to stop. And, reaching the gelding, "Wellman's in town, Tom. His daughter's missin', and he's lookin' fer her."

"What's that got t' do with me?"

"They say she left right after you and Matt were out there this mornin'."

For a moment McBride let his stern eyes touch every watching face, and then he went along the boardwalk and into the jail.

Pat Loomis was talking to Harding, the banker, who stood with his back to the door. The stringy, slightly bent deputy glanced at McBride, his bright eyes cautious, but his long, sunhardened face was expressionless.

"Been waitin' fer you, Tom," said Loomis. "Matt'll be back in a little while. He wants to talk to you."

The banker swung around. He was dressed neatly in a black broadcloth and held a small leather bag. There was a tense nervousness about him McBride could sense. "You were out to Arrowhead this morning, McBride. Did you see Helen when you left?"

"Will Dundee just told me she was missing," McBride said shortly. "She couldn't've gone far."

"That's what Wellman thinks," Pat Loomis said. His careful eyes watched McBride. "Matt went down to the hotel and boardin' house to see if she's in either place."

"That's probably where she is," McBride said.

"Matt thought you might know."

McBride shrugged. "How would I know?"

"You might've bumped into her on the road," Loomis said.

The banker added, "Wellman's put up five-hundred for anyone who finds her." He patted the leather bag. "Five hundred's a lot of money, McBride."

A little flush came into McBride's face. He stared at Harding and said, "Even if I knew, I wouldn't do anything about it for the money."

"Well, I just thought..." Harding stopped talking as Bonham and Wellman came into the office. Behind the rancher Harry Dean followed. When he saw McBride, he stopped tensely, his bandaged head held stiff and dark eyes flickering nervously.

Matt Bonham walked to his desk and sat. He rubbed a hand wearily on his jaw. The lack of sleep showed in his thin face and bloodshot eyes. "Did Helen Wellman pass you on the road today, Tom?" he asked.

"No. Hell. Mat, you were with me."

Wellman took off his sombrero. He said in a thick angry voice, "Dammit, she went out right after you left. I want her back. You know anything, you tell us right now."

Bonham stood and walked to beside Wellman,

looking smaller next to the big rancher. "I'll do everything I can to find Helen, Lew," he said, "but I won't stand for any gunplay."

"There won't be." The rancher's anxious eyes shifted to McBride. "I don't want trouble," he said. "I want my daughter back, that's all."

Wellman called off his gunslicks, he thought. It meant that much. Helen was the weakness the ranchers could hold over him.

"She wasn't at the hotel or boarding house?" Harding asked.

"No," Bonham said. "She's not in town."

Harding said, "Sheriff, would you make sure the word gets around about this reward." And, as if he'd suddenly made a big decision, "I'll add five hundred myself. You can pass that around, too."

Bonham was thoughtful for a few seconds. "I wouldn't be too worried, Lew," he said. "She was all excited about you hitting her. She'll get over it and go home. She might be back there now."

"If one of the ranchers or settlers haven't got her," Harding offered.

McBride saw the excitement and concern in the banker's face. Harding wasn't in the same state of mind as Wellman. He was scared, and the five-hundred he'd put up was part of that. But why?

"I'm going looking if she isn't back," Wellman said, his voice stiffening. "And, I'm starting with Double F. You come along, Matt?"

"Sure," Bonham said quickly. "But, it won't be a posse. There won't be any searching ranchers without their okayin' it."

Wellman stared at him. "I'll be in at daybreak unless she's back at the house."

"All right," the sheriff said. "Don't worry. She'll turn up."

"She'd better, Matt," said Wellman, his voice calm.

"Bonham knows what he's doing," Harding said. "Anyway, the reward'll bring someone in with information." His stare was on Wellman, warning him to keep quiet.

Wellman put his sombrero on his head. "I'll get her back," he said tightly. He hesitated a moment, as though he meant to continue, but, catching the banker's look, he said no more. He turned and went towards the door, and Harding followed.

Bonham stared at their backs. He had seen the look, too, and stood thinking about it. He motioned for Pat Loomis to follow them out. When McBride started to leave, he spoke up.

"Tom, you'd better tell Crashaw we're comin' to Double F. I don't want the whole thing set off 'gain."

"I'll ride out first thing in the morning," McBride said. Then, he told the sheriff about what he'd seen at the line camp.

"Damn it, I should've figgered Wellman would use a place like that," Bonham said. "But to prove a case against him we've got to have Eyester himself."

"We could check on the other places Wellman bought up. Maybe..."

"No," the sheriff said, as if mentally bothered by something. "Wellman's all through giving trouble, Tom. He'd get Eyester off his land. He knows someone'll take it out on the girl if there's any more trouble."

"Then, it might be a good idea if Wellman worried a little longer about the girl."

Suddenly, Bonham said, "How do you figure Harding in on this, Tom?"

McBride hesitated. "I don't know. But he was as worried as Wellman."

"You think the girl knows anything?"

"She might. Look, what're you going to do when you find her?"

"Make her go back, if I can." He rubbed his hand wearily over his chin. "I'd like to know just how deep Wellm'n and Harding are, but I don't think talkin' to her would do any good. She wouldn't hang her father."

"She could let something slip without realizing it," said McBride.

"Not to me. She'd be damn careful what she said to me." Now, Bonham stared at McBride. "You know where she is, Tom?"

"I'm going to find her," McBride said. "When I do, I'll talk to her."

Bonham nodded. "Well, be careful. I'm not sure Wellm'n actually is the big man in this. So, you be damned careful, Tom."

THIRTEEN

McBride took a room at the hotel that night. After two days of little sleep, every muscle of his body strained, his eyes smarting in protest from staying open. But he slept uneasily and was up before daybreak, his mind mulling over what he might learn from Helen Wellman.

He reached the Linford ranch just before seven. No one was in sight when he pulled up, but as he swung down to the ground, a voice called to him from the barn, a sharp voice that had an edge to it.

"Keep your hands where I can watch them, mister."

He didn't move his hands from the saddle horn. Facing the barn, he saw Susan Linford coming out the half-opened door. Standing there at the big building she seemed awfully small. The .45-70 Winchester she held made him aware of how helpless she actually was, and he felt suddenly sorry for her and wished she would listen to him, or let him help her.

"I surrender," he said, raising his hands, shoulder high, and grinning.

"What're you here for, McBride?"

"I want to talk to Helen."

She lowered the rifle. "I didn't recognize you coming down the trail," she said.

"Well, I'm glad you aren't trigger-happy," he said drily.

He told her about Wellman calling his men off. "You won't have to keep that ready anymore," he said.

Susan shrugged her shoulders. "I'm not putting it away until I'm positive about things."

The remark bothered him; it was simple and direct, with little hope in it. He started for the porch. "All right to talk to Helen?"

"She's getting dressed. She'll be out in a few minutes."

"Everything go good?"

"Yes. She's a nice girl." Susan stepped up onto the porch and looked at him, shaking her head. "Helen's all through with her father. She says she won't go back to Arrowhead."

"Wellman's calling everything off, just to get her back."

Susan was silent. She looked pale and tired, and he realized rather abruptly how fine her features were, that she'd lost her little girl look and now seemed very much a woman.

"Helen told me about how you tried to stop the trouble," she said softly. "I'm sorry I acted like I did. I wasn't sure of you, and I couldn't take any chances."

"I didn't get anything accomplished," he said bitterly. I couldn't ever get your father to listen to me."

"My father had such big plans for this ranch. It meant so much to him."

"He was a man all the way," McBride said. "There's nothing to be ashamed of here, Susan." His words were reflective and sincere, and he saw a truth in them he hadn't seen before; now, he knew the wrong in the hate he'd felt since Big Bend for people like Ed Linford, who'd fought and loved and died for a purpose, standing up under the constant pressures from the land and men.

"It's all such a waste," she said in a low voice.

McBride nodded slowly. So damn much waste, he thought. He groped for something to say, wanting to know this woman better and to be closer to her.

The front door opened and Helen Wellman came out. She was dressed like Susan, but the soft blonde hair long about her shoulders, made her seem much more feminine. She saw McBride and smiled.

"You seem to be around all the time, Tom." She laughed quietly. "I'd've run out with Sue if I knew it was you."

"There won't be any need for running," he said. "Your father's called his men off. He wants you back."

Helen stared at him. "I'm of age, Tom, and I won't go back there. Sue said I could stay here until I decide what to do."

McBride saw Susan's nod. "You should go back. He's sorry, Helen. I've never seen him so broken up."

"I don't know," Helen said, shaking her head. "He might begin the trouble again once I'm back at Arrowhead."

"No," McBride told her. "He's got too much to lose. He's even put up a reward for anyone who had information about you. And Harding put up five-hundred, too."

"Harding?" Her eyes darkened. "Did he know Dad was calling off his men?"

"Yes." He watched her, seeing her mood change. "He was pretty worried, too. You'd think he was part of the family by the way he acted."

She rubbed her hands together, not answering.

"Why would Harding offer so much, Helen?"

Quickly, "He's a good friend of the family. And Dad does all his business through the bank."

"That mean he should put up money?" he said. And when she still kept silent, "Just how close is he to your father's business?"

Helen stared at him nervously, held by his hard eyes. "There's something of a partnership," she said. "Dad doesn't make a move unless they talk it over."

"You sure Harding isn't the one who's boss?"

Her eyes flickered. "Dad made his own decisions. He's been wanting to buy up all the land in the Basin ever since I was a little girl."

"But why all the trouble now? Burning and killing good men. Why does he go to that length now?"

Helen's eyes filled with tears. "I don't know, Tom. I still can't believe Dad's behind it all. I..."

"He is, and you know it," he said, cutting her short. "And if you know anything, you should tell the law."

Susan Linford said suddenly, "McBride, you're not the law, and you haven't any right getting after her like this."

He turned to Susan slowly. "Can't you see that if Harding's the boss, the trouble might not really stop now?"

"I can see you're bullying her," Susan said sharply.

"Good Lord. Your father was killed, I thought you'd be sensible enough to understand."

"Leave her alone," Susan said. "If she knew anything, she'd tell you. Can't you see that?"

112

"Well, you'd best hide her," McBride said. "Wellman's going to visit the ranchers today looking for her."

Helen said then, "You won't tell him I'm here." He saw that she was close to tears.

"I won't tell him." He was silent a moment. "But you remember. You stay here, there may be worse trouble than before."

At that, Helen turned and went inside, and quickly returned, holding an envelope in her hand.

"I wrote this to Dad," she said, holding it out to McBride. "It tells him I'm safe and explains everything. He'll understand. Will you mail it from town?"

For a moment he stared in silence. "You're sure you want it this way?"

"I know I do."

McBride nodded and pocketed the letter. He climbed onto the black and rode from the yard. A little more than an hour later he came onto the ranch lane leading to the Double F. Hot sunlight already made the air heavy beneath the trees lining the trail, and changed to a burning disk as it struck his body once out of the shade. The men guarding their small herds in the meadows turned to watch McBride with solemn eyes. They'd be able to relax now, he thought. Frank Crashaw would pass the word quick.

The front door opened and Crashaw came onto the porch when McBride entered the yard. Frances, following her husband, stopped in surprise when she saw McBride dismounting then come towards them.

"You're way off trail this mornin'," Crashaw

113

said. "I heard you were lookin' fer Wellm'n's girl." He walked to his edge of the porch and stared down with tight eyes.

"Wellman's got enough men hunting for her without me," said McBride.

"Heard 'bout thet, too," Crashaw told him. "Seems like Matt Bonham's givin' Wellm'n a real free hand, lettin' him look through every place in town. And the bank offerin' a big reward, too. Seems like they're givin' him every bit of attention a man could get."

"Matt only let him look in the hotel and boarding house."

"I heard different," said Crashaw, shaking his head and ignoring McBride's statement. "And, they tell me, there's a posse gonna search every spread in the Basin."

"The sheriff's riding with Wellman. They're not going to search any place unless the owner allows it."

"They won't search this ranch," Crashaw said, his mouth hardening slowly into a flat ugly crease.

"Wellman's fired his gunslicks. He's through making trouble," McBride explained, and waited calmly.

"For now," Crashaw said.

"No. For good, if you work along with him." He was staring at the look of hope that had come into his sister's eyes. Maybe she'd help out now. She was the only one who could control her husband. "I came out to tell you they'll be here soon," McBride said. "Let them look around if they want to, and let Wellman see you're with him on this. That's the best thing you could do."

"So, you're back on his wagon," Crashaw said

thoughtfully. "If you are, you're a damned fool. You can't appease Wellman. Haven't you learned that yet?"

"There won't be any appeasing."

"You don't think so, eh?" Crashaw shook his head angrily. "We all want to believe everything'll straighten out jest with a snap of a finger. But it can't be. You can't wipe clean a slate that shows four ranchers burned out and two damn good men dead. You can't just raise your hand and expect the dead cattle to come back. Face the truth, at least, Tom, he made a damn fool of you, keepin' you runnin' 'round like a messinger. Don't think people don't know how he uses any excuse to git his way. We're not the damn fools Wellm'n thinks we are."

"All right," McBride said quickly. "But just let them look for the girl. She isn't here, so you've got nothing to lose."

Crashaw looked at him in silence for a few seconds, all the tense patience fading slowly from his face. "Wellm'n's lucky he'll have a law man with him, or he'd never step foot on my land."

"Listen, Frank. Try to understand, will you?"

"No. I've got work to do." He started down the steps towards the barn, eyes still on McBride. "Wellm'n should be damn glad I don't give him the same reception he promised anyone who came on his land. You rem'mb'r thet."

When her husband had gone, Frances Crashaw said, "Come on inside and wait, Tom."

McBride nodded, watching Crashaw, who was now standing near the wide-open barn doors talking to Ben Huntoon. Then, McBride went inside the cool, dim living room.

"You can't expect Frank to forget so quick,"

Frances said. "He's got to be careful, with everyone else lookin' to him for what to do."

"That's just why he should let Wellman look around."

"Well, maybe he'll think about it," she said, a bit hopefully, McBride thought. And, as if she'd suddenly made up her mind about something, she crossed behind him and left the room.

Frances soon returned and stood at the curtained window, her tall body rigid as she stared down the trail. For a moment McBride watched her silently. "Frank change his mind?" he said, finally.

"No." She glanced at him.

He said nothing.

"Frank's right," she said suddenly. Her voice was high and thin, a tremor of fright in her handsome face. "He's doin' what he thinks is right. If Wellman's really sincere, there won't be trouble anyway."

Loud footsteps sounded on the porch and McBride turned. The front door opened and Ben Huntoon came in.

"They're ridin' in," the young cowhand said. "There's four of them all t'getha. Frank says t' come out."

"We'll be right out," McBride said.

McBride's mouth tightened. "Ben with you or Frank?" he said as Huntoon left.

"This is Frank's ranch now, Tom. He wouldn't keep Ben if he didn't agree." She spoke calmly, but her face was antagonistic. McBride could see she expected an answer about the ranch being Frank's. They were still worried about that, too.

Shrugging his shoulders, McBride moved towards the window. He heard the faint sound of hoofbeats. Stopping beside his sister, he looked through the curtain. Wellman and Matt Bonham were coming into the yard first. Behind them, Harding and Brazos rode in single file. McBride moved towards the door, but when Frances spoke, he hesitated.

"Rememb'r," she said, "Frank speaks for hisself."

He nodded. "He'll have to this time."

She opened the door and stepped out on the porch, and McBride followed her. The group pulled up near the house, and Wellman and the sheriff dismounted. Frank Crashaw was at the barn saying something to Huntoon, who nodded; then the rancher came across the yard, his shoulders squared and bearing aggressive.

"Mornin', Franny," said Matt Bonham. The sheriff turned his attention to Crashaw as if he was simply making a casual visit to pass the time of day. "Lew's daughter's bin missin' since yesti'd'y mornin', Frank. You hear anythin' 'bout where she could be?"

"No." Crashaw's voice was sharp, unfriendly. He glared at Wellman.

"We're checkin' every ranch," said Bonham. "Mind if we look around?"

"Yeah. I do mind."

A moment of silence followed. Wellman started to say something, but Bonham motioned him quiet with his right hand.

"I don't want to have to force anything, Frank," he said.

"Sheriff. You got one of them legal papers that says you can search my place?"

"I didn't think I would need one."

Color rose in Crashaw's cheeks. "You do, Sheriff," he said slowly. "I'm tellin' you the girl ain't here. Either you take my word or go git thet paper."

Wellman had been listening with his tired eyes staring from one face to the other. Now, he cleared his throat, and when he spoke his voice was patient. "You can see we're not looking for trouble, Crashaw. Helen's missing, and I've got to find her."

Crashaw looked at him contemptuously. "That's too bad. You should've worried 'bout somethin' like this happenin' 'for you started burnin' and killin'. It's too damn bad thet..."

Bonham stopped him with a gesture. "Hold on, Frank," he said. "You won't let us look here, that's one thing. There's no call for startin' trouble."

Crashaw took an involuntary step forward. "I'm the one that's startin' truble? You fergit what's gone on the last few months, Sheriff?"

"This is a different matter, Frank."

"Okay, you've got my answer then," said Crashaw quietly. "You'd better ride."

Harding had moved his horse up close to the porch. Crashaw didn't immediately notice him, until the banker spoke. "I told you that you wouldn't get anywhere this way," he said to Wellman. "Crashaw knows where Helen is all right, but this isn't the way to handle him."

There was something new, a trace of pain on Wellman's face. "I called my men off," he said to Crashaw. "I fired those guns I hired to protect my land."

"So, what do we do about what's already done," said Crashaw sarcastically, "fergit it?"

"Frank, I'm sorry for anything..." Wellman began, but when Harding cut him off, he silenced quickly.

"We're going to find the girl," the banker said. "If you know anything, you'd better tell us." There was an angry glint in his wide black eyes, but his round mustached face was otherwise expressionless.

McBride was sure now that there was something Wellman feared from the banker that overshadowed his concern for his own daughter. McBride watched Harding, a bit amazed at the cool, arrogant way he dared to show his hand. It was very important they find Helen Wellman, perhaps more so to the banker than her own father. But why?

Crashaw moistened his lips. "You'd better ride out," he repeated, then turned and started towards the barn.

"Well, what are you going to do, Sheriff?" said Harding.

"She ain't here. We'll ride," Bonham said abruptly.

Harding shook his head disgustedly and muttered something under his breath to Wellman, but the rancher didn't seem to hear.

"But, we'll keep looking?" Wellman asked Bonham as he took hold of his stallion's reins. "We've got to look."

"We'll look," Bonham said. He climbed into the saddle and, glancing once more towards the barn, wheeled his horse and started moving alongside Wellman. Harding and Brazos followed.

Frances Crashaw turned to McBride. "You think it'll begin all over again?"

"I don't know."

She hesitated, then said, "He did what he thought was right, Tom. There are too many people to think of. Frank couldn't let them down."

"Franny. That didn't help anyone. You know that."

She didn't answer.

McBride hesitated a moment, and then he went across the yard to his black. He had to find out more about the banker. Helen had left a lot out, he knew, yet it was doubtful she really knew the whole story. He rode slowly from the yard and headed his mount for Cavanagh to ask some important questions.

FOURTEEN

The bank was a two-story wooden building with an overhanging porch set appropriately next to the sheriff's office. Inside the air was close. McBride went directly to the teller's window and stood waiting for Martin Douglas to finish some work at his desk.

McBride pushed his sombrero back and mopped the dust he'd collected riding in from his forehead. "Hot day," he said to get the teller's attention.

Douglas turned and looked at him, then stood. He was about sixty, a slender, pale man with a Lincoln beard hiding most of his narrow face. "What you say?"

"Warm," McBride said again.

The teller shrugged his shoulders carelessly. "Suppose you want the money Arrowhead owes you."

"There's no rush. I can wait."

"No bother. I've got it right here," Douglas said and turned towards the desk. When he returned, he pushed a sealed envelope out beneath the iron bars."

"Young Huntoon hasn't been in for his money," the teller said absently. "You tell him it's waiting for him."

McBride nodded. "He might be going back to Arrowhead," he said, "now that the trouble's stopped."

"Mister Harding wouldn't advise Wellman taking either you or Huntoon back."

McBride looked at him interestedly. "You think he'd take Harding's advice?"

"He always has."

"Yeah... with their being in business together, I suppose Wellman has to listen to him."

Douglas wet his lips. "What business is that?"

"Oh," McBride said, gazing absently at the picture of the president, "I worked at Arrowhead long enough to know Harding has a hand in Wellman's land buying."

The teller's face changed as if he'd been struck. McBride's hope of learning anything here died as he stared at the frightened bearded man. For a few seconds there was no sound but the ticking of the wall clock.

"You've got your money," Douglas said shortly. "Anything else I can do for you?"

McBride stared at him coldly. "No. I'll tell Huntoon his pay's here," he said and turned towards the door.

Outside, he mulled over his next move. Then, McBride remembered he had Helen's letter, and he went along the boardwalk to the Overland Express Office.

The agent wasn't there, but the clerk, a big, dark man about McBride's age, named Pooley, was sitting behind the waist-high counter that ran the length of the small room. His visor was pushed back on his round forehead and a thin Mexican cigar jutted from his mouth. He looked drowsy and comfortable, as if he were about asleep, but he grinned when he saw McBride.

"Hi, Tom. Long time no see," he said and puffed contentedly on his cigar.

"I've got a letter for Wellman. Put it in their pile." He laid the envelope on the counter.

The big clerk stood leisurely, taking the cigar

from his mouth. Watching him, McBride had a sudden idea. "Wellman gets lots of mail these days, don't he?"

"He gets his share, Tom."

"I heard some talk about there might be copper in the Basin," McBride said. "People've been wondering about that since they struck ore out in Humpback."

Pooley was silent a few minutes. He nodded slowly. "That's close to two-hundred miles away, but I sup'ose there could be ore almost anywhere."

"Just some talk I heard. I figured you'd know if Wellman got any business mail from an ore company."

The clerk turned and took some letters from one of the cubby holes lining the back wall. "Only one who gets lots of business mail is the bank," Pooley said without looking up. "You know how it is with a bank: they hear from everything—stocks, bonds, railroads. You know."

McBride watched him in silence. "I guess they'd buy up a lot of railroad stock."

Pooley shrugged. "Get a lot of mail from them, anyway," he said. "Mister Harding gets three, four letter a week hisself, lately."

There could be something in that, McBride thought, and then maybe not, for a banker would have his hand in a lot of things. But he'd talk it over with Bonham. There was no short cut to finding out just exactly where Harding's connection with Wellman was. You could only try every lead.

"Nice seeing yuh again," he said to the teller.

"Thanks. Nice seeing you, too, Tom."

McBride started towards the livery stable,

uncertain about everything. Then, he stopped and stared at the hitch rail in front of the jail. Matt Bonham's stallion was racked in its usual place. He went quickly into the office and was told by Pop Holmes that the sheriff had just gotten back and was eating at the Dutchman's.

Crossing the street, McBride went quickly along through the hot sunshine to the restaurant. Bonham was sitting alone at a table facing the window of the large dining room. McBride sat down next to the sheriff.

"Thought you'd be out most of the day, Matt."

"Post 'an Gruber wouldn't let us look either. Tomorra we're goin' out with papers an..."

"That could cause more trouble, Matt."

"I'm goin' t' ride out to see Crashaw this afternoon," he said. "He's the one holdin' things back, now."

"You'll have to be careful with him," McBride said, doubtful. He leaned closer and told Bonham what he'd learned at the stage office.

"Could be somethin' to it," the sheriff said. "I'll wire the capital and ask 'bout that."

"It could explain why Wellman wanted all that useless land, too."

"How do you figure that?"

"If the railroad's planning on building through here, whoever owns the whole Basin could ask his own price."

Bonham nodded, rubbing his boney chin. "Damn it, Tom, first thing I want is to get the girl back to Wellman.

McBride hesitated. Then, he said, "He'll know Helen's allright by tonight."

Quickly. "How d'ya know?"

"There's a letter from her at the Overland. It says she's safe, and it explains everything else."

"You knew where she was all along," Bonham said, his voice crisp. "Why didn't y'tell me?"

"She made me promise I wouldn't. She's all right, Matt. She's..."

Bonham cursed softly. "Damn it," he demanded, "don't you realize that Wellman could've turned this basin upside down lookin' for her. I thought you were working with me, Tom. But you're so damn sure you're the only one c'n handle things, y'took a chance on ruinin' everythin'."

"Nothing's happened, Matt. And, she would've refused to go back to Arrowhead anyway."

"You play square with me," Bonham said bitterly. "You go git thet girl and bring her in t' me. Then, I'll send fer Wellm'n. I went them t' talk it out 'tween them."

McBride pushed his chair back. "I'll try, Matt."

"You git her in here," Bonham said tensely.

McBride went out of the restaurant and down to Sinclair's Livery for his horse. Sinclair was in the small darkened office he'd built on the right side. He glanced at McBride when he entered, his long, pallid face watchful, as if he was afraid of something.

"I'll saddle Cloud," McBride began. "Don't bother..." Now, his voice broke off as he heard the movement behind him.

McBride turned and saw the hulking shoulders of Harry Dean, and beneath his bandaged head the glowering face closing in on him. Young stood behind the giant, blocking the door. McBride was completely unprepared for anything like this, and every muscle in his body began tightening. Foolishly, his hand began moving for his gun.

Young's hand snapped down and up, the complete movement taking only an infinitisimal fraction of a second. "Keep 'em high, jasper," the stubby gunman said.

McBride stood motionless, a lump in his throat.

"Heard yuh've been askin' questions 'round town," Young said. "You're too damn nosey, jasper."

McBride was silent. Harry Dean was beside him now. The huge man worked quickly, unbuckling and jerking the gunbelt from about McBride's hips.

"Where's the girl?" Dean said.

"I don't know."

"Let's get goin'," Young said. "Fergit the girl. We'll find her." He leaned against the door. "Yuh better stop askin' questions, jasper. You'll git hurt that way."

"Harding getting worried?" McBride said.

"Jasper, you're a damn fool," Young said, smiling as if amused. Then he nodded to Dean.

McBride did not have time to turn before he felt the driving fist smash down on the back on his neck, the blow snapping his head. He began raising his arm to ward off the next blow, then felt the stinging viciousness of Dean's powerful punch ripping his nose wide open.

Dean's voice came from what seemed a long way off. "Where's the girl?"

"I don't know," McBride mumbled.

Again a smashing blow landed, and another and another. McBride's legs gave out and he reached out to find something to hold onto. He slid to his knees, the chopping fists still pounding his pain-racked head. Then, one of them began kicking him. He heard some voices, the rumble of loud laughter; shortly, a blackness of nothing surrounded him, and silence stopped all the pain.

FIFTEEN

McBride opened his eyes and looked around, then tried to get up off the bed.

"You stay theah an' git more rest," Nate Antrim said from near the window. He came over and stood by the bed, looking down at McBride's swollen and discolored face, the large bandage covering the cut right ear, puffed lips and the purple bruise that ran from chin to the black almost shut, right eye.

"How long I been here?"

"Since two-thirty...moren' five hours. They gave you a bad beatin'."

McBride remembered now. He raised his right hand and dubbed at the dull pain and stiffness in his face, but then dropped it again and lay back, dozing. He didn't feel connected to anything except the soreness in his head. Suddenly he opened his eyes and half sat.

"Anybody get Dean, or Young? They did it, Nate."

"No." Antrim still looked tired, his mustached face slack, and he had a coarse dark stubble of beard. "You wuz lucky they din't kill yuh. Would've if old Sinclair wasn't theah."

"How'd I get here?"

"Will Dundee told Bonham to bring yuh heah."

That's where he was...Dundee's house. McBride slid to the edge of the bed and started to stand. His head began throbbing steadily and his weak legs wouldn't hold him. He sat, glancing about. A small clock said ten-to-eight.

"Bettah rest awhile longer," Antrim said,

watching him. McBride fell back on the soft pillow and then, after a few moments was sleeping again. Two hours later, he woke, looked around for Antrim and saw the cowhand wasn't there. He could hear talking downstairs, low, muffled voices. He felt hungry and sat up. Then, he stood. His head still throbbed and legs weren't very steady; so he held onto the iron end of the double bed and stepped slowly to the water pitcher on the dresser.

The water stung his face but helped bring him around, strengthening him. The voices had moved out into the street and were no longer distant. He crossed to the window and saw a number of men and women standing in the street, talking excitedly.

He looked around when he heard the door creak open, and Nate Antrim came in.

"How's the head? Yuh feelin' bettah, Tom?"

"I'm all right. What's going on out there?"

"Killers hit agin. Dynamited the Linford ranch house," Antrim said, and McBride felt himself tremble. "They killed Miss Helen. Pat Loomis's gone aftah the body now."

"Good Lord! What about Susan?"

"She's okay. She shot Eyester from the bahn. They jest brung 'im into town."

McBride took a long slow breath of relief that Susan was all right. He splashed more water into his face and then put on his gunbelt. He went slowly out of the room and downstairs. The crowd at the door opened a way quickly for him. Pop Holmes for once wasn't whittling, and he stared at McBride's face. Susan was sitting in the swivel chair at the desk. She stood, clenching her hands tightly when she saw him.

"Tom," she said, taking a long slow breath. "What happened?"

"I'm all right." Quickly now, "What did they do out there?"

"Helen's dead."

"I know. Tell me about it." He saw it was an effort for her to keep herself steady. Her thin face was white and strained, and her lower lip shook slightly. "Take it easy now," he said. He pulled the chair up to her, and, taking her arm in his hands, nodded for her to sit. "You were in the barn, weren't you."

"Helen wouldn't come out. She got to joking about my running for the barn every time I heard a horse. I went out anyway." Susan breathed in deeply and a little shiver shook her small body. "It was about an hour after sunset. The rider came across the meadow and up close to the house. I thought it was you, Tom. He was tall and sat straight like you do. Then, he threw something and began riding hard, and then the explosion came."

McBride glanced toward the people crowding the doorway. "You got Eyester."

"Yes. Frank Crashaw brought us both into town. The sheriff took him over to the doctor's." Her arm became tense. "I wish I'd killed him. I do, Tom."

"You recognized him then?"

"He's the man who killed my father."

McBride squeezed her arm and she looked up at him, her eyes moist. He felt deeply moved and groped for something to say that would help.

Frank Crashaw pushed through the crowd, half-dragging Eyester behind him. Ben Huntoon and Antrim came in just ahead of Sheriff Bonham, who halted momentarily to speak to the watching townspeople.

Eyester stopped in the middle of the small room. His shirt was opened in the front and there was a large bandage covering his chest. He rubbed his face and stared at Susan Linford, his eyes filled with the wild hate of an animal.

"Didn't figure on the barn," he said finally, as if reluctantly admitting the girl had outsmarted him. "That was something I didn't figure on."

"All right," Crashaw said, holding the iron-rimmed door leading to the cell block. "Inside!"

Bonham walked to beside Eyester. "You're goin' t' hang," he told the killer. "Why don't you tell us who you've been workin' fer?"

"I won't be in here long," Eyester said.

"Who're you workin' for?"

Crashaw said, "He's workin' fer Wellman. Dammit, we all know that."

The small sheriff shook his head. "Wellman wouldn't have taken a chance on killin' his own daughter," he said and stared into Eyester's calm face. "It'll help at the trial if you talk. You'll damn well hang if..."

"I'm tired. Don't you know I got shot? I want to sit down."

"Use your head," Bonham said. "Tell us who's behind what you did tonight."

Eyester gave him a quick, ugly laugh. "I'm tired, Sheriff. I told you that."

Bonham suddenly pushed the killer's shoulder hard, starting him toward the cell block. Eyester shouted an obscene curse.

Susan shook her head slowly. "How can a person be like that, Tom?"

"It's a form of insanity. But, it's no worse than the man who hired him."

Susan hesitated, then said, "I didn't imagine it could happen. I'd've made Helen come out into the barn."

"You aren't to blame. The fault's more mine for taking her to your place."

"She was so happy because her father had called his men off," Susan said, pain clear in her face as she looked into his eyes red with exhaustion.

"Where'll you go?" Tom asked.

"The Crashaw's want me to stay at their ranch."

Bonham and Crashaw came out of the cell block.

"Matt," said McBride, "you need Susan any longer?"

The sheriff rubbed a weary hand over his forehead. Shortly he said, "No. She can go." And to the girl, "I'd like to talk to you in the mornin'."

Crashaw said, "Franny's waitin' for you at our place, Sue." He looked over at Ben Huntoon. "You take her out there?"

"Sure."

McBride put his hand gently on the girl's slim shoulder. "I'll come out and ride in with you tomorrow. You wait for me."

She nodded, then stood and went out with Huntoon.

Frank Crashaw looked at McBride's face and said softly, "They did a good job on you, Tom. Dean and Young, I heard."

McBride tried smiling, but the smile didn't come

off because of the puffed lips. "They figured they owed it to me."

"Wal what d'ya say?" Crashaw asked. "I think Dean and Young high-tailed it straight to Arrowhead. We can ride out there and finish this trouble once and fer all."

The sheriff stood silently pouring tobacco into his pipe, then lit up. After a few puffs he took the pipe from his mouth. "I don't think Wellm'n was behind this," he said bluntly. "He told us he fired Dean and the others, and I believe him. Anyway, they'd stear clear of Arrowhead. Now that the girl's dead, they'll have Wellm'n t' answer to."

Crashaw's expression remained doubtful. "We should take Wellman in," he said. "He was the one who hired Eyester in the first place."

"I'm goin' out to git him later."

"You'll need a posse," Crashaw said quickly. "With all you got 'gainst him, he won't come in just by askin'."

"Don't you worry 'bout thet none. My job's takin' him in, I'll take him in."

"Just like that. Face the facts, Sheriff. He could git a lot tougher, now that his daughter's dead."

"I'll ride out with you, Matt," said McBride, breaking through the tension. "We'll take Helen's body back there and..."

Crashaw interrupted. "Don't be a damn fool. You'll both be killed."

McBride studied his brother-in-law's hard, impassive face. "Wellman's been out of this fight since the girl left him. But, once he learns she's dead, if there's a posse after him, he might start fighting all over again," he said.

"We take Wellman in it'll all stop anyway," Crashaw said.

"Don't be so sure." Bonham frowned thoughtfully at the rancher. "Stopping Wellman won't end anything."

McBride asked, "You get an answer back from the capital?"

A silence expanded in the small room, broken only by the noise of people somewhere outside in the streets. "You were right," the sheriff said at last. "The railroad's plannin' on runnin' a spur line through the Basin to that ore strike out in Humpback. That's why Wellm'n wanted every foot of land. He began rushing things 'cause they were goin' t' start buyin' rights in September. There's even some talk that *Great American* is plannin' on puttin' a smelter up, too."

Crashaw was hunched a little forward, his face grimly excited. "So, we get Wellm'n an' finish him up now."

"He isn't in it alone. I take him in an' I've got to spill my hand to whoever's in it with him."

"At least it'll stop the killin' and burning'," Crashaw said.

Bonham was about to answer when the noise outside became louder. Then the door opened and Pat Loomis entered. The stringy deputy gestured toward the street and said, "I got the girl out there, Matt. Think you'd better take her out to Arrowh'd fast."

McBride followed the sheriff to the door and looked outside. The townspeople were crowded around the wagon just beyond the boardwalk. Someone held up the canvas covering to see the body. Faces were grim and frightened, but the atmosphere had changed. There was a rising anger mixed in with the tension and excitement. The sheriff backed away from the door and said to Crashaw, "You git back out t' your herd."

"I'm goin' to Arrowhead."

"Damn you, you do what I say! You want to see Franny laid out like that?" And, when Crashaw stared at him, breathing deeply, "You watch your own place, and have Huntoon spread the word fer everyone else to keep their eyes open."

He took his sombrero from the desk and walked out, motioning at McBride to follow. The talk died down suddenly, only a few voices in the back keeping on. Boots sounded on the boardwalk, and there was loud clopping of a horse trotting along the road.

"Get this gang broken up," Bonham said to the deputy.

Loomis nodded and began moving the people back.

The sheriff lifted the canvas, his face expressionless. McBride came in beside him and stared at the torn figure a moment, his face shocked and grim in the leaping light slanting through the jail windows. The dynamite had gone off right close to her. She couldn't have felt a thing, he thought. For another moment, McBride stared at the singed yellow hair, keeping his eyes away from the rest of her, the pulpy mass of black and white and red that had been her body.

"We'd better get her out of here," he said to the sheriff.

Bonham glanced around, sensing the temper of the mob. They weren't simply discussing this any longer, but were worked up, ready for a lynching.

Many of the men carried guns, and there were more horses moved in close, their waiting riders looking too quiet, too determined. "You'd better git your horse, Tom," Bonham said.

A rider yelled, as if Bonham was a long distance off, "We're with yuh, Matt. Yuh want a posse?" And more voices echoed his.

"There'll be no posse," Bonham told them. "I'm takin' her back to Arrahead. You people move 'long now."

"You'll need help. Wellman won't come in after this."

"Move 'long now," Bonham said sharply. He got up onto the wagon seat and then looked down at Loomis. "No one follow us, Pat. You see t' that."

Someone yelled hotly. "We don't want our wimmin' 'n' kids blown up like thet, Matt. We want t' finish this right t'night."

Bonham glanced around, his face unpleasant. "Pat," he said to Loomis in a loud voice so everyone could hear, "you shoot the first man who tries t' follow. You got thet?"

Catching the deputy's nod, the sheriff started the wagon off. The townspeople moved from his way hurriedly. McBride came out of the livery stable drawing his black on the bridle, and seeing the departing wagon, mounted and rode slowly through the mob. He came alongside the canvas-covered figure, and then slowed the animal to keep pace with the vehicle.

Close to two hours later they saw the lights of Arrowhead ahead of them and shortly turned into the long, tree-lined drive. Wellman had heard the squeaking wagon coming and was standing on the veranda, waiting. He wore an undershirt and jeans, seeming thinner, and no longer formidable; he was simply a tired, worried man who naturally hunched his shoulders.

The rancher glanced at McBride; and, he straightened suddenly and caught his breath, his wide eyes glued to the discolored, battered face.

"Brazos said you'd been jumped, McBride," he said, not changing his expression. "But I want you to know I didn't have anything to do with it."

"I didn't figure you did, Mister Wellman."

Wellman's eyes shifted to the rear of the wagon, resting on the canvas. "What you got there, Matt?" he said.

"You'd better come down here, Lew."

"If it's any trouble, I'm not to blame." Wellman walked down the steps grudgingly, his face annoyed.

Bonham came around to the rear of the wagon, stepping in beside McBride, but he hesitated before pulling back the canvas.

"Well, what do you want?" Wellman asked anxiously.

The sheriff looked into the bigger man's face. "Eyester dynamited the Linford ranchhouse tonight. Helen was inside. She's under here."

"Dynamite?" Wellman stared at him, unbelieving. "It couldn't be," he mumbled. His face was white. "They couldn't've done any more dynamiting. He said they'd stop." He shook his head slowly. "No. You're wrong, Matt."

"We got Eyester, Lew. But Helen's dead." He raised the canvas enough for the rancher to see.

Wellman stared, dumbfounded. His lips trembled and he reached out with both hands and held onto the side of the wagon. He muttered something inaudibly, and then his wide shoulders began shaking.

Bonham dropped the canvas back into place. McBride reached up and began lowering the tail gate. At the rasping sound of wood rubbing, Wellman looked up. His eyes were wet, but he had complete control of himself.

"You got Eyester?" he said.

"Yes. Susan Linford shot 'im from the barn."

Wellman shook his head. "Harding said he'd hold them off 'till I got her back." His voice was hoarse. "He promised he'd hold them off."

"Then, the trouble was goin' to start again," Bonham said.

"He promised he wouldn't start up again 'til Helen was safe." He reached up with his right hand and touched the dirty, rough canvas tenderly.

Bonham said coldly, "You should've been smart enough t' keep it stopped. You should've made sure Harding stopped."

Wellman looked at him. "I couldn't hold him. It was his plan. He had those gunboys hired for me."

"You'll have t' come back t' town," Bonham said. "I want the whole story, right from the time you herd 'bout the railroad comin' into the Basin."

"You know about that?"

"All about it," Bonham said. "I want Hardin' though. You're goin' t' put everythin' into writin', Lew."

Wellman bit his lip as he stared into the sheriff's hard eyes McBride watched the big rancher, feeling no pity for him. When Wellman had others in this position, he'd showed no pity. He'd been alone with his own grief now.

"Rememb'r, Hardin' had Helen killed," said Bonham.

Wellman's eyes rested on the canvas. "I'll give you everything you want," he said bitterly. "But once you get Harding, you'll have to cover me from Dean and Young. They're bad ones, Matt."

Bonham nodded. "Get Wellm'n's horse, Tom," he said. "We're goin' back and finish the whole bunch off, and we'll start with Hardin'."

SIXTEEN

It was after two but ahead in Cavanagh a few lights were still burning. The buildings seemed like irregular dark shapes bunched up in the flat.

They rode at a jog, McBride and Wellman just ahead of the rumbling and squeaking wagon. He threw a glance at the tall rancher, seeing that Wellman was still leaning forward a bit in his saddle, thoughtfully quiet, as he had been since they'd left Arrowhead. McBride looked ahead, feeling a quiver of excitement along his body. It was close to being over; but you couldn't be too sure. Harding had cleverly handled the whole thing so far, and now the banker wouldn't just stand around and be taken in.

The rifle shot came at that moment, followed instantly by a low grunt from Wellman. McBride's reaction was instinctive: he was off his horse, his Colt in hand, taking a fraction of a second to break Wellman's fall to the ground.

Bonham's small figure moved beside him with the speed of a cat. "It came from the feed shed," he said, gesturing to the right. The only sound came from his hands as they groped over Wellman's body. "Dead," he muttered.

McBride studied the dark row of buildings a hundred yards away, mostly sheds and store-houses of the town's merchants. He could see no movement.

"I'll try to get them into the open. Take the left," Bonham said. Without waiting for an answer, he began running across the street toward the feed shed, and suddenly he disappeared into the shadows.

Moving quickly out wide on the flat, McBride ran to the rear of the closest building and made his way circuitously along the cross street cutting onto Grant. In the cover of the porch he halted. There was no noise or movement close by. Carefully, he went onto the porch, certain he could cover anyone the sheriff drove out.

A shot sounded from somewhere behind the feed shed, then two more quick blasts echoed along the alleyway. Then silence. More yelling toward the center of town. People were already in the streets.

Two figures broke from the alleyway halfway up Grant and went along the boardwalk. Suddenly the bigger man started across the street. McBride aimed his Colt but then dropped it, knowing that because of the townspeople behind the running man, it was too long for a safe shot.

He ran along the walk, his bootheels pounding on the boards. Ahead, the figure vanished into an alley. McBride slowed and peered around the corner before following. He caught a blur of movement at the further end and managed to pull his head back before a slug gauged a long furrow along the shingles, showering splinters onto his sombrero. Then, he caught a hint of motion near the poplar trees lining the small creek.

He threaded his way past the wood-pile and, crouching lower, got through the trees and into the muck at the edge of the creek, his boots squelching at every step. Minutes later, he knew he'd lost his man.

In the shadow of the hotel he halted, feeling

tense and cheated at missing his chance. He returned his gun to its holster, and glanced along the street.

Most of the town was up, and people still boiled out into the street.

Bonham stood on the opposite walk, and, when he saw McBride, he crossed the street. A half dozen people crowded around, flinging questions to which the sheriff paid no heed.

"Lost mine, Tom," he said, "but I think I nicked 'im."

"Missed mine, Matt."

The sheriff glanced around as if calculating his next move.

"Someone shot Wellman," Bonham said. "We were bringin' 'im in."

"He's dead?" someone called from the crowd.

Bonham glanced at McBride, his eyes warning. "Don't know. I'll go git 'im." He spoke loudly so the onlookers could hear.

McBride looked around, feeling the excitement. When his eyes reached the hotel steps they stopped. Harry Dean was standing there, a small grin on his mouth as he watched McBride's bruised face. McBride stared the huge man up and down. His look froze when he saw Dean's boots had drying mud around the heels and toes.

Dean's grin faded as McBride mounted the stairs.

"What d'ya want, McBride?"

"Why'd you shoot Wellman?"

Harry Dean sniffed and breathed in deeply. Neither man moved. Finally, Dean's flat voice said, "I was inside 'sleep when I heard shootin'. I came out t' see what's goin on."

"How'd you get that mud on them boots?"

The giant gazed down at his feet. Scowling, he shifted his weight. "I was down by the crick 'bout a hour 'go." He spoke pleasantly, but there was an edge to his words. "Look, McBride, I wanna git back t' sleep." He turned and went toward the hotel door.

McBride followed him inside. "Hold it, Harry!"

Dean swung around, his face openly hostile. McBride was sure now. Dean said, "Look, ask Lawson, here, if I wasn't in all night?" He walked to the desk and looked at the little clerk. "You tell McBride I was in my room when the shootin' started."

"Sure...he was in his room." The clerk edged back from the desk. A slender, pale man of about forty, the thinness of his face accented his fright.

"See, McBride, I got a witness." Dean waited patiently.

McBride didn't take his eyes from the huge man. "Lawson, you'll go to jail," he said, "if you lie for him. If Wellman's dead, it's murder, and you're lying, you'll get mixed up in it," he said.

The clerk moistened his lips. He said slowly, "I don't want no part of it."

"A man can hang for shielding a killer," McBride said. He saw Dean's right hand lowering, so he dropped his own down and touched his gun, and the clerk saw that, too. He could read the promise in every line of Dean's massive body, in the narrow, violent eyes.

"I'll go down to the jail," the clerk said, his voice pinched. He started to come out from behind the desk, but stopped like he'd been hit when Dean said, "Stay there. McBride ain't no law man."

There was no sound but the clerk's quick breathing.

Shortly, "I'm not hanging for you," he began. "I..."

"Okey," Dean said quickly, "we'll go see Bonham." He hunched his big shoulders as if he were starting forward. McBride saw the movement and began reaching for his Colt. His hand slapped down and then up, firing as Dean's gun cleared the holster. Dean's body stopped moving, a growing blotch of blood darkening his shirt's right side. McBride's .44 roared again, the bullet tearing into Dean's shoulder, and the huge man's gun fell heavily to the floor.

"Get the sheriff," McBride ordered the clerk.

Dean, flushed with desperation, flung himself at McBride, his uninjured arm swinging out and hitting with a staggering force. McBride kept his balance, then brought his left up with a short, vicious hook that doubled Dean over. He banged the flat edge of his palm down on the back of the gasping man's neck, and Dean crumbled to the floor.

"Who was with you?" McBride said.

Dean stared at him, hate shining from his eyes. "Ya got the wrong man, McBride," he said.

"Who was with you?" McBride repeated.

Dean continued to stare at him, saying nothing.

McBride swore. He'd had enough of the whole weary business. He wasn't dealing with a man; they were all vicious inhuman animals who killed at will.

He swung the Colt down. Dean jerked his head back from the blow. His lips opened partly in a glowering snarl, but mostly from fright. The iron barrel struck a glancing blow on the fleshy left cheek, tearing it open and knocking Dean into the wall.

"You're going to hang for the killings," McBride said, grabbing the front of Dean's shirt, yanking him to a sitting position. "Every damn one of you're going to hang."

"What? I didn't do no killin'."

McBride slapped Dean's face three, four times, mercilessly, and tears came into the wide eyes. "Linford and Paulson were damn good men," he said bitterly. "You tell me all about Harding's part in it." And seeing Dean's expression go blank, he slapped him again. "You talk, damn you, or I'll kill you right here!"

Dean's lips trembled, staring into the muzzle of the Colt. "Hardin' planned everythin'. I'll talk," he whispered. "Jus' don' shoot." He wet his lips. "I din' want no part of killin' Mistuh Wellm'n. Young did it, anyways. I din' shoot nobody."

"Why'd they want to shoot him?"

"Hardin' was 'fraid he'd come lookin' fer him. He din't know the girl was inside that settler's house, or he wouldn't've had Eyester blow it up. He couldn't explain it was a mistake to Mistuh Wellm'n, though."

"I'd think he'd of been satisfied killing Linford without going after the girl, too."

"He figgered the settlers'd quit once her place got hit again."

McBride felt the shock of realization. They could try for Susan again. "Where's Young?" he asked.

"He went to Hardin's place. They're each other's alibi."

Footsteps hammered on the hotel porch. The door pushed open and Bonham came in.

"Young bushwacked Wellman," said McBride,

145

glancing from Dean to the sheriff. "Harry was there, too. He says Harding's behind it."

Bonham said, "You willin' t' go all the way on this, Harry?"

Dean paused, looking up at McBride, the complete fear still in his face. "Yeah," he answered. The fright faded a bit then, replaced by nervousness and worry. "Look, I din't kill nobody. If I help now, will yuh talk up fer me?"

Cautiously, Bonham said, "It won't hurt."

"They're goin' t' hit Double F at daybreak," Dean said. "Young an' me were goin' in with 'em."

"How many of them are there?"

"Four. All gunboys Hardin's brung in."

A surprised and shocked gasp went up from the onlookers.

"You want a posse, Matt, I'm with you," a man yelled. More voices joined in.

Bonham said to some cowhands close by. "Take Dean over to the jail. And tell Pat to start formin' a posse." Then, the sheriff turned to McBride. "You come with me, Tom. I want Hardin' locked up 'fore we leave."

"Young's there, too, Matt."

Bonham pushed through the crowd and onto the porch. McBride was right behind him. Harding's big house at the east end of town was lighted. Together they started toward it, the anxious crowd following at a safe distance. Nate Antrim caught up with McBride and fell in alongside him.

"Where in hell you going?" said McBride, dropping back a step.

"I wanna be in on this." The lanky cowhand had lost his worried ways. His right hand was held just above his gun.

McBride hesitated. It was what they needed, but

Antrim wasn't the man for it. "Get back with the crowd!" he said.

"No. I'm goin' t' be in on it."

"You'd better ask Bonham."

Antrim shook his head quickly. "They made me hide in thet room, remembah? Everybody thinks I'm yellah. I gottah prove somethin' to myself and to them. Yuh see, Tom?"

"Keep behind me then," McBride said, tensely. Now, he walked faster, half-running to catch up with the sheriff.

Harding was watching them approach from his long veranda. The banker stood as if lounging, his mood one of studied casualness which might have amused McBride if he was more sure of how it would all end.

He followed Bonham through the gate in the white picket fence, past the big cottonwood on the lawn to the bottom of the steps.

Bonham's voice was loud, firm. "I'm takin' you in, Hardin'. Keep your hands high and come down here."

The banker's calm expression didn't change. "You don't have anything on me, Matt. Wellman's the man you wanted. I was told he's dead."

"I got Harry Dean down at the jail," Bonham said. "He had a lot to say 'bout you bein' back o' the trouble in the Basin."

Harding's small eyes wavered. He threw a hasty glance to his left, seeming startled. He hesitated. "I don't know what Dean told you," he said finally, "but he's lying about me." He was calm again.

McBride tensed up. Harding would bluff right to the end. And, he was clever. They could lose him after all. "Where's Young?" he said.

"How should I know?" The banker looked at

Bonham. "Sheriff, I'll talk to you, but I don't have to answer this cowhand's questions."

"Dean said Young killed Wellman," McBride's voice shook. "He said Young came down here."

"He's a liar."

Bonham looked into the house. "If you're in there, Young, you come out with your hands up." His voice echoed clearly along the quiet street.

There was only silence from within.

"I told you he wasn't here," Harding said. "I'll gladly come to your office, Sheriff. You'll see Dean's a damn liar." He started forward abruptly to come down the stairs.

Bonham said to McBride, "You watch Hardin'. I'm gonna have a look inside."

People were stirring in the street. McBride took a step toward Harding. A shot suddenly came from somewhere in the house.

McBride half-turned away from the banker. Two more quick gunshots sounded, behind the house this time. Harding seeing the group's attention shift from him started to run, but he stumbled and fell down on the lawn.

McBride ran to him. "On your feet!" he ordered.

Harding was kneeling now, swaying a second, and he looked around at the townspeople. "Yellow coyote," a man called. Fear masked the banker's face. He began straightening up, keeping close to McBride.

Someone behind McBride screamed a warning. "The corna of the house! The corna!"

McBride swung about, his hand going for his Colt. He saw Young clearly then, standing there on the lawn at the end of the porch, blazing six-guns in his hands. McBride's gun was still not clear of its holster when something struck his side, spinning him around and staggering him backward. There was an immediate searing pain that drove him to his knees. He heard two shots pound close by, on his left. He looked up and saw Nate Antrim standing in front of him, looking as tall as the cottonwood. People shouted loudly, confusedly.

"Yer okay, Tom," Antrim said. He held his gun on Harding who held both arms high about his head, a bright flame of terror in his eyes.

McBride suddenly felt as if he were going to vomit. "Damn good work," he said, and the pain made him moan. He glanced down the length of the porch and saw Young lay prone and motionless. A glaze came into McBride's eyes.

"Here, you men," he heard Bonham say, "get his legs. You, take his head."

McBride felt a flash of dizzying white-hot pain as someone gripped his shoulder. He looked at the sheriff. "They're gonna hit Double F, Matt," he said.

"We're ridin' out now, Tom. You take it easy there."

"Sure," said McBride. He began trembling all over, his stomach filling with nausea. Glancing at Antrim, he saw the cowhand was busy reloading the fired chambers of his six-gun.

"Thanks, Nate," he said.

SEVENTEEN

Young's slug had glanced off a rib and furrowed a small hole along McBride's side. Doc Cooley cleaned the wound, rubbed in some ointment and bandaged it snugly. McBride felt washed out and empty and slept nervously most of the morning in the iron double bed in Dundee's sparsely furnished, clean bedroom. Afterward, with the strength coming sluggishly back into his body, he sat up, making and smoking cigarettes in chain-like fashion.

Will Dundee came in shortly before eleven. "Posse's comin' back," the fat saloon-keeper said. "Got all four of 'em, Tom. Killed one, I think."

McBride got slowly to his feet and began dressing. He had his jeans and shirt on and was finishing with the buttons. He sat on the edge of the bed. "Help me with the boots, Will."

Annie Dundee was standing in the open front door when McBride came down the stairs a few minutes later. "You shouldn't be out of bed," she said. Then, noticing McBride wore no gun, the thin woman's soft eyes became bewildered. "You think it's safe to go out like that, Tom?"

"It'll be safe to go without a gun from now on, Annie."

"Well, just remember you can stay here as long as you want."

"Sure," said her husband. "You come back here, Tom."

"Thanks." McBride was going to say more about how much he appreciated all their help but something in their faces told him they understood. "Let's see how things went, Will."

The street and walks in front of the jail were crowded with people. At least fifteen horses were racked at the hitch rails nearby, a large group gathered around a pinto from which Pat Loomis and two cowhands were taking a dead man's body.

McBride saw Crashaw and Nat Antrim talking to Bonham at the desk. Susan Linford, her face drawn and tired, stood silently near them. She saw McBride and looked at him, her stare anxious and intimate somehow.

Bonham started for the cell block but hesitated when he noticed McBride. "We're gonna git their stories on paper," he said. "You wanna come inside, Tom?"

"In a minute." McBride went to where Susan stood. "How come you're here?" he asked her. "You didn't get hurt, did you?"

"No. The sheriff wanted to take down my statement. How's your side?"

He stared into her pale face. "Oh, I'm okay. You look tired. You ought to sit down."

Susan nodded. He asked Will Dundee to get a chair. "Franny isn't here," McBride said. "She all right, too?"

"She taking care of Ben. He was the only one who got shot. Not too bad, though."

Susan sat and McBride looked down at her. "You're going to be around for awhile, aren't you?" he asked.

"Yes, Tom. You should go back and lie down." Her glance shifted from his shoulder to the dark bruises on his face, and her lips tensed in anger.

"I will." He smiled at her, feeling moved. It was suddenly intently important she stay there until he came back. "I'll see you in a few minutes," he said.

She nodded. "Don't stay up too long, Tom."

He walked past the heavy iron-rimmed door and into the small cell block. From the last cubicle, Eyester, his long, sharp face pressed close to the vertical bars, studied the group crowded around Harry Dean. Harding and three men McBride didn't recognize watched from the other cells. Dean lay on his cot talking to the sheriff and Crashaw. Pooley, the clerk from the express office, wrote hurriedly and steadily across a big paper pad.

Nate Antrim came up beside McBride, the cowhand's face shining with pleasure and confidence. "Too bad yuh missed the fight, Tom," he said. "Din't last long, but we ended the trouble roun' heah once and fer all. All's we did was wait out in the meadow an' them gunboys rode right into our trap like we'd sent an invite. Hey, how's youh gunshot, Tom?"

"All right." He looked along the line of cells as a loud string of curses came from Eyester, the tall killer swearing at Dean for talking so freely.

Antrim grinned. "Matt's not takin' no chances on Harry's changin' his story. He's sendin' to Jensen Hole fer the judge. Wants to finish the whole thing up quick."

McBride felt the weak tiredness coming back. "Tell Matt I'll be over at Dundee's house if he wants to talk to me."

"Suah, Tom."

Frank Crashaw left Dean's cell and stopped beside McBride. "Wal, we got everythin' straight now," he said. His strong face was still tired but the tenseness was no longer there. "Soon's the

152

trial's over, we'll give 'em a quick hangin'."

"Lucky to get them all at once like that," McBride said.

"There was no luck to it." Crashaw exhaled heavily and rubbed his chin. He looked into McBride's eyes. "I was waitin' fer 'em t' hit my herd anyways," he said.

"Yeah," Antrim said. "Frank had Benny and Waco Evans out with his herd, too."

"If I'd've taken your advice, Tom, I'd've lost some of 'em."

McBride's mood changed. He looked at Crashaw and said, "Heard Franny's taking care of Benny."

"Ben and Susan'll be 'round 'til they git straightened out."

"Franny'll be pretty busy," said McBride.

"We'll all be pretty busy." Unconsciously, Crashaw glanced at McBride's wounded side.

McBride studied his brother-in-law for a few moments in silence, a bit irritated that Crashaw was feeling him out about his wanting to go out to Double F. Then he said lightly, "It'll be good to work again without worrying, won't it?"

"Without worryin'?" Crashaw said wearily. "The way things are, there'll be lots to worry 'bout. Always somethin' you c'n worry 'bout when you run your own spread. You been workin' fer Arrah'd so long you're forgettin' what it's like."

"You'll do all right, Frank."

"I'll keep right on like I bin doin'," Crashaw said quietly. "I figger I can keep Ben on, and we can handle it."

"Sure." McBride knew the worry about his

claiming his share of the Double F was still there. "You and Ben'll keep it going good," he said impersonally, so Crashaw could see he had no worry. Now that the trouble was over, he really hadn't thought about Double F; but he was very certain he'd never work for or with someone else again.

Bonham came down the aisle, and he stopped beside Crashaw. "I got all I need," he said confidently. And to Pooley behind him, "Take down the girl's statement." He smiled awkwardly. "Not too sure these'll stand up in court, but I figger it'll stop Dean from changin' his story."

"I must've been a damn fool not to see what was going on," said McBride.

Matt Bonham shook his head. "They were clever 'bout it, Tom. Wellm'n kept them gunboys hid all the time. Only when it looked like real trouble, he decided to bring Young and Eyester to Arrahead. That's why he fired you, so you couldn't put two an' two togetha."

"Harry say who bushwhacked Dawson?"

"He don't know." Bonham frowned. "One of the hothead ranchers could've done that. I'm goin' t' check on it."

"How about the gunslicks?" McBride said. "They talk?"

The sheriff rubbed his boney jaw and said wearily, "No. They got some kind o' code they stick to. Can't figger 'em out."

"Their damn code won't do 'em no good when they feel their necks in a noose," said Crashaw.

McBride stared at the cells. So, it's all over, he thought. The prisoners didn't look at all dangerous, but now were only silent unimportant men

154

who didn't matter any longer. Yet, they'd changed his existence completely.

"What about Arrowhead and the ranches Wellman bought up," he asked.

Bonham shrugged. He hesitated and said, "There's no relatives I know of. Judge'll have to handle legal end o' things."

Crashaw said then, "You thinkin' of buyin' a spread, Tom?"

"Don't know. Figure it's about time I got a place of my own."

"Mebbe they'll go for taxes," Crashaw said hopefully.

"We'll see," Bonham said. He swung the iron-rimmed door back and went into the office. Pat Loomis was clearing the mob of onlookers away from the door and only the old jailer was in the small room, besides Susan and Pooley. McBride waited another five minutes, while the sheriff talked to the girl. The heat increased his tiredness. He sat in a chair, his body feeling drained and hollow. When Susan started to leave he went outside with her.

They walked to where Crashaw's buggy was parked. Susan hesitated at the step plate and stood with her hand touching her temple, studying him.

"What's wrong?" he said.

"You should be lying down."

"I'll be all right," he said quietly. He felt awkward, not sure how to go about this. He looked into her small, pretty face, wanting to say something he couldn't put into words. "You're going to stay at Double F," he said finally. "Frank said you were."

"Yes. I'll be all right."

"You're going to rebuild, I suppose?"

"I'll have to. It won't be too hard, once I have a shack on the ranch."

He saw Crashaw come out of the jail and stop on the walk to talk to Pat Loomis.

"My side'll be okay in a few days," he said, the words coming slowly, as if speaking was an effort. "I'll be riding out there then."

She looked at him thoughtfully. "You don't want to rush it too much. Let your side heal up before you do any riding."

McBride nodded. Crashaw's footsteps pounded on the boardwalk behind them. She got up onto the seat and sat there with her feet set firmly on the floorboards. Staring up at her, McBride saw how calm her serious face was.

"I want to ride out to see you," he said quickly.

"I'd like that." She smiled into his weary eyes and touched his discolored right cheek lightly with her hand. "But you've got to rest a lot before you do," she said.

Frank Crashaw went around to the other side of the buggy loudly.

Susan turned to look back, and McBride waved. He watched her until the buggy turned south onto a side street. For a few more seconds he kept staring; then he turned and walked slowly toward Dundee's little white house.

Steven C. Lawrence was born Lawrence Murphy in Brockton, Massachusetts. He was educated at Massachusetts Maritime Academy and earned a Bachelor's degree and Master's degree in journalism at Boston University. For thirty years he taught English in Brockton. He began his career as an author of Western fiction with *The Naked Range*, published in 1956 by Ace Books, followed by two of his most notable novels, *Saddle Justice* (Fawcett, 1957) and *Brand Of A Texan* (Fawcett, 1958). He is perhaps best known for his Tom Slattery series, beginning with *Slattery* (Ace, 1961). In this first book, Slattery returns from five years in a federal prison after being framed for a crime he didn't commit. After avenging himself, Slattery went on to a new adventure in *Bullet Welcome For Slattery* (Ace, 1961) in which he gets involved with smuggling over the border between Texas and Mexico. Some of the best entries in this series are *North To Montana* (Nordon, 1975) where Slattery faces treachery in Calligan Valley at the end of a long cattle drive and *Day Of The Comancheros* (Nordon, 1977) where Slattery finds a woman raped, beaten, and left to die in the desert. Generally, the Steven C. Lawrence Western novels, as George Kelley noted in *Twentieth Century Western Writers* (St. James Press, 1991), are "filled with thrilling adventures based on historical fact and solid plotting.".